Carter

Enjoy when you are not hitting tennis balls.

Hope you enjoy as much as I did writing it.

Best

HILDY'S PROMISE

Richard M. Finn

Cover art credit - Jacqueline Sweet

Copyright © 2023 Richard Finn

All rights reserved.

Acknowledgments

On the surface writing a book is a solitary project. The author sits at the computer typing away at the keyboard for hours alone. That is far from the truth. There are so many people supporting and encouraging every author and every book. I have tried to thank the ones who helped me.

By luck and good fortune, I reunited with Julie Ward, my former editor at USA Today. Julie is the best editor and colleague a sportswriter and author could ever want. There would be no book without her tireless work. All typos and grammar errors are mine and mine alone. Thank you, Julie.

To my mystery writers' group, good friends, and aspiring writers all Andrea Colby, Van Wallach, Steven Parker and Lynn Samaha. Thank you for all those zoom meetings, your encouragement, and suggestions.

To my friends from White Plains, Jim Weinstock, Raul and Nancy Ortega, Evelyn Petrone, Donna Menin, and Diane and David Schonberger thank you for so many years of being together. An extra shout out to David who got me playing golf.

To Andrea Siede a member of the family and of that younger generation who can do almost anything on the computer and does, thank you.

And finally, to the three most important people in my life – Andrea, Stephie and Jackie – all my love.

For Julie, who made it a better book.

– CHAPTER 1 –

THEY came in with guns drawn. There were two of them. Both wore Halloween masks. Bishop was Donald Trump complete with hair. Thornton wore a Chucky mask also with a shock of hair. Both wore latex gloves and even booties on their sneakers.

It was a little past noon on a sunny spring Sunday in the New York City suburbs when they surprised her in the spacious kitchen preparing lunch.

She was dressed in a short sleeveless pink dress, with buttons down the front, which showed off shapely and toned legs with curves in all the right places. At 52, Hildy Swanson was still a looker.

She dropped the salad tongs on the floor and looked at the intruders with shocked surprise.

"If she moves, kill her," Bishop barked to Thornton. Then he shouted at Hildy, "Where's your phone? What's your password?"

After she pointed to her cell and gave them the password, they hastily gagged her and sat her down at the kitchen table. They took her photo with her phone, scribbled her password on a piece of paper next to it and then left it along with a manila envelope addressed to "Mr. Cassidy" near the unfinished salad.

Bishop took out another blank piece of paper and a black sharpie. He put the paper on the table and gave Hildy the sharpie. Her hands were shaking.

"Write what I tell you," he ordered.

When she was done Bishop took the paper. They tied up her hands, walked her out of the well-appointed five-bedroom, four-bathroom colonial with the requisite pool and patio in the back, out to the circular driveway, past the Mercedes and Mini to a small black Honda. They bundled her in the trunk, got in, took off their masks, gloves and booties and drove off.

The entire encounter took less than fifteen minutes.

In the car, Bishop reflected on Hildy's short dress and her curves. Not bad, not bad at all for an old broad, he thought. Nobody had told him he couldn't mix business with a little fun he thought.

As they drove out neither man noticed the security camera perched on a tree at the bottom of the driveway

* * *

About 90 minutes later RG Cassidy returned home from Sunday tennis practice with his club's Westchester County Tennis League (WCTL) Open division team. They were preparing for the next weekend's championship match against Pleasantville Tennis Club, and it was a hard and spirited workout. He had a grey Oklahoma State tee-shirt on and white Adidas tennis hat. At 37, he was in pretty good shape—five feet ten, about 165 pounds —with light brown hair and brilliant blue eyes. He had an engaging smile and plenty of women thought he was good-looking.

After playing tournament golf as a youth through college and even taking a swing at making the PGA Tour, Cassidy had picked up tennis about six years before, finding that his native athletic prowess made him exceptionally well suited to the game. A smattering of lessons had helped enhance his performance and now he was one of the better players at the club with a coveted singles spot on the club's very competitive WCTL league team sprinkled with several former college players.

He headed into the kitchen for a cold drink. That's when he saw the uneaten salad and the envelope. He opened the envelope. The ransom note was typical in that it was printed on plain white paper. Its message was not.

We got your wife. Check out the phone

Bring $300,000

Trencher's Farm Golf Course

Tomorrow at 1:00

Tee time in your name

18 holes match play

Win and you get your wife back

Lose and we keep her for more money

No tricks No cops Be there

He saw the phone. Opened it. Saw the photo of Hildy trussed up and sitting right where he stood now at the kitchen table. Then he searched everywhere—inside and outside the house—calling out her name all the while.

– CHAPTER 2 –

THE getaway had gone clean and smoothly.

Thornton did the driving, keeping the car well below the speed limit and obeying all of the traffic signs.

Bishop and Thornton had rehearsed the route several times before so there were no surprises. The route kept them out from downtown Cable Springs and most of the congested areas. They never saw a cop.

In the blackness of the damp and dirty trunk, Hildy was scared and frightened. Her hands were tied, she was gagged, and her legs scrunched up. She was shaking and tried to take deep and slow calming breaths.

She knew that they turned right out of her driveway. They were going over paved roads and there was not a lot of stopping and starting so she guessed that they were not going through town. But other than that, she had lost a sense of any direction.

About 30 minutes after leaving the house, Thornton turned right onto a sparsely populated gravel street with several sprawling horse farms set far back from the road on each side.

The road got bumpier, and Hildy was jostled around in the trunk, once almost hitting her head on the top. She even thought she heard a horse whinny. Dirt began to seep into the trunk and she felt some cold air rush up under her dress and she tried to keep her legs closed out of modesty and warmth.

After passing a woman on horseback slowly trotting on the road, Thornton turned up a rutted dirt driveway that was overrun with vegetation. A battered sign hung off a wooded post at the turnoff.

Coarse Gold Farms

Bishop wryly smiled at the name.

The car bumped around and they could hear the woman grunt after one bad bounce. Up ahead was a worn down two-story house that was partially hidden by a row of trees. Off to the right was an old two-car garage its doors wide open and ideal to stash the car out of sight. An equally rundown barn stood off on the left.

Thornton stopped the car in front of the battered farmhouse.

They had been told that the property had been empty for months and there was little chance of them being disturbed.

Before Bishop and Thornton had arrived two days ago, they had stopped at a big supermarket about an hour away to buy food, water, liquor, bathroom supplies and a box of latex gloves. They had packed sleeping bags with them in the car and had put them upstairs in two rooms. At a big hardware chain store, they got flashlights and several candles as the electricity had been shut off months earlier.

They put on their masks and tucked their guns in their pants. They took a look around, saw nobody and popped the trunk open. Hildy looked up into the sunlight, blinking her eyes as they adjusted. Hands tied. The little dress hitched up well past her knees. Helpless and all ours thought Bishop.

Bishop reached down, making sure his hands ran across her breasts as he yanked her out of the trunk.

"I will take her in," said Bishop, holding her up. "You get the car into the garage."

He quickly blindfolded her before she could get a look around. Then he hustled her up some creaky stairs, shielding her with his body just to be extra careful that nobody might catch a glimpse of her from the road.

– CHAPTER 3 –

IN a well-kept two-story house on a quiet tree-lined street, Cable Springs Police Captain Charlotte McBain was in her backyard grilling Sunday lunch of burgers and hot dogs for her husband Bill, 7-year-old Steven and 5-year old Stella.

McBain was juggling making a family favorite meal and talking with her father Pat. The phone call started with the kids talking to Granddad before McBain gave her father a recap of her ongoing investigations.

McBain welcomed her father's thoughts and insight accumulated from his 40 years as Police Chief of the small Vermont town Barre before he retired five years ago to tend to his wife Elizabeth in the final stages of her fight against cancer.

Her father was the reason the 42-year-old McBain and only child of a solid middle class family had pursued a career in law enforcement picking Northeastern University in Boston and its strong Criminal Justice Program before getting a spot in the Vermont Police Academy in Pittsford and then starting with the Burlington (Vt.) force.

In the two years since joining the Cable Springs force, her case load had increased as the once sleepy little town about 40 miles north of New York City grew into a busy suburban town with all of its accompanying troubles of drugs, robberies, and even killings.

"You are keeping real busy these days Charlie," Pat said using her family nickname.

"And the last active case is the Mendoza gang slaying. That's the one where a local merchant and his wife were mutilated and she was raped in the attack," said McBain.

"Sounds like a nasty one, who's your lead," asked her father.

"Detective Garrett and his partner Judd. They are my most senior pair," said McBain.

"Garrett, didn't you have issues with him when both of you worked in the High Country?" said her father.

McBain was silent for a moment.

"Yes, I still feel a bit of tension around him," said McBain. "But, back to this case you know their deaths remind me of the killing of the prostitute and her boyfriend by her pimp when I was in Burlington. You remember that one don't you Dad? That is where I met Chief Morton."

There was silence on the phone for a moment.

Benjamin Morton, High Country Sheriff Office chief, was the second most important person in McBain's career. He had become her mentor during the years she spent Upstate. Nowadays, McBain still frequently got his advice on particularly difficult cases.

"I don't remember that one too well, go back over it for me Charlie," said her father.

In vivid detail McBain told her father about the murder 12 years ago when Morton literally walked into her life.

McBain and her partner were the first to respond and found the boyfriend near the front door she remembered. He was naked and lay face down in a pool of blood.

A naked woman was in the next room on the bed on her back. She had been cut wide open from her chest down to the bloody patch of pubic hair. But the most horrific act the killer had done McBain would never shake from her mind.

Jammed into the woman's mouth was a severed penis, that McBain could only believe came from the boyfriend by the front door. McBain just hoped that she had been already dead when she was brutalized. And that he too had been dead when he was mutilated.

"Morton was there, never noticed him but guess he noticed me," went on McBain. "We were there for about an hour going over the murder scene with the detectives and ME (medical examiner) collecting evidence. Later that day, I met with Morton and he offered me a position and promotion working directly under him in the High Country office in Upstate New York."

"Now I remember, " said her father.

"Two weeks later, I packed up my old yellow canary Jeep from school and headed up north. That's where Morton would teach me and where I fell in love with Bill," said McBain of her husband of nine years. "And also ran into Samuel Garrett."

Before hanging up, McBain told her father that she loved him, and would speak next week.

– CHAPTER 4 –

AT that moment, Detective Samuel Garrett sat on a threadbare couch in his tiny apartment above the hardware store a few miles away on the town's main street.

The blinds were closed to the brilliant afternoon sunshine as for the last two hours, the three-year-veteran of the Cable Springs police department had been staring intently at the NBA game on TV with a bettor's desperate hope in his heart.

Clutching a beer, he muttered, "Come on boys, do daddy a favor here. Come on boys no fucking foul."

But there was a foul, two foul shots swished through the net, the wrong team won, and Garrett lost $500.

Garrett closed his eyes. "Fuck, fuck," he said, tilting his head back and gulping down the rest of his beer.

* * *

Garrett had good intentions when he decided to be a cop, following in the family tradition of his uncle John who had a distinguished 25-year career on the Buffalo force.

Uncle John would tell him that as a cop you were doing your community and your neighbors something good, especially when you put the bad guy away. As a kid Garrett would simply sit and soak it in. By the time he was in high school he knew what he wanted to be.

It was with little surprise or fanfare that after graduating from college, he passed the police exam and got a job in the High Country sheriff's office.

During Garrett's nearly five years Upstate he did a little bit of everything – traffic tickets, patrolling the towns and parks, breaking up drunken fights, domestic abuse, drugs, prostitution and the occasional robbery and homicide.

He also did a lot of betting.

Garrett had always been a sports junkie. Sports Center. Monday Night Football. Game of the Week, March Madness, if it was on he watched it. He lived and breathed it as a kid.

When he turned into a betting junkie was a little bit harder to pinpoint.

Maybe it was at college when he started laying off $20 and $25 bets with the guys down at the town bar on games.

Baseball, NBA, NHL, Triple Crown, March Madness and of course football, pro or college. It didn't matter. If they were keeping score, if there was a winner or loser, he was betting on it.

By the time he arrived in the High Country he was hooked. He needed the adrenaline rush of the bet, the excitement of the action, and the high of the win.

The problem was that he was not a good bettor. He fell $5,000 in the hole and on his salary, he might have been a million dollars in the red to have any chance of paying that back without a huge winning streak.

A hard guy named Albert Harrigan ran the bookmaking operation. In fact, he ran all of the criminal activities in the area including girls, drugs, and guns.

Harrigan was street smart and tough but had moved up to fancy suits, luxury cars and an expensive house out on the outskirts of town. Garrett had seen what Harrigan had done to people who crossed him or couldn't pay up debts. Garrett knew that even his sheriff's badge wouldn't protect him.

Harrigan ran his business out of an old farmhouse called the Ranch. Both were accepted part of life in the High Country. Still, once in awhile the law had to make a show of force.

"The DA is up for reelection and she wants to make some headlines, "Chief Morton told his officers in the briefing room one fall morning. "She wants us to raid the Ranch and grab some headlines. It will be all hands on except for our office desk staff. We go on Friday, two nights from now, so the place should be busy."

* * *

On Friday night, a steady rain mixed with a little sleet fell out of a dark, starless, and moonless night when the police rode up in unmarked and silent cars and stopped at the bottom of the Ranch driveway. But the lights were blazing at the Ranch and cars filled the gravel parking lots.

Before heading up to the house and barn, the cops pulled out shotguns and officers checked their Glock pistols. They silently all gathered around the Chief, who quickly gave out orders.

"Garrett, you and TC take the back entrance," Morton said. "McBain, you and the others come with me and go up the front. We go in on my signal. No wild cowboy stuff. We want to put people in jail tonight, not into body bags."

The Ranch was a collection of structures on an old horse and hen farm about five miles out of town. The main house was an old fashioned two-story house with a large front porch that extended around to one side. On the ground floor there was a big poker room with three tables sometimes in action simultaneously, along with an Old West fashioned parlor and bar where the girls hung out and mingled. A big stairway to the second floor was lined with paintings of nudes and semi-nudes on the wall.

Upstairs was Harrigan's office, with an armed guard outside at all times. A room with TV monitors with feeds coming from the security cameras scattered around the grounds and staffed 24 hours a day was next to his office. His bodyguard Potts was always nearby.

While the main house had a couple of bedrooms reserved for the wealthy clients, the old barn had been reconfigured into a series of small bedrooms on the floor and even in the loft for the girls. An armed bouncer sat at the doorway. The hen house had been turned into a storage facility for the guns and drugs and was guarded day and night by two armed guards.

Harrigan was in his office sipping expensive Scotch, smoking Cubans and talking with the Mayor of a nearby town who was waiting for his favorite lady when he got the call from his security office that the police were heading up the driveway.

Most nights Harrigan would have gone without a fuss, chalking it up as a simple nuisance and part of doing business. A single phone call now would have his lawyer at the station before he even got there and out within hours.

But this was not most nights and he really was given no choice.

"I can't be here, if they find me here it will fucking ruin me," said the ashen-faced Mayor. "You got to get me out of here and quick."

Harrigan got up from his desk. He left the Glock in his desk. He had learned that it was better if he didn't have a weapon on him if the police picked him up. Plus, he was a businessman now, not a thug.

"Got a back way out of here, and car waiting outside. Move quick Mayor. Potts, the bookcase," Harrigan yelled at his burly guard who stood nearby.

Potts easily moved the bookcase off the wall to reveal a stairway. Harrigan turned on the flashlight and stepped in the lead, motioning with his head for the Mayor to follow.

"Potts close it up and follow," he said. Downstairs he could hear noise and loud voices.

They made their way quietly and quickly down to the cellar. Harrigan led them across the basement and then up a couple of steps leading up to a storm door.

Outside it was a slow slog to get around to the back for Garrett and TC through the mud and slippery ground with not much light. Just as they turned the corner, three men emerged from the storm cellar.

It was hard for Garrett to see who exactly the men were with the rain and sleet blurring his vision. He took a glance at TC and motioned with his hand to move up quickly.

"Stop, police!" Garrett yelled.

The three men looked back to see who was yelling. At the far end of the building, Garrett could make out a car.

Two men stopped and turned. The person on the right kept on running. The one on the left reached into his pocket and brought out an object. The one in the middle stood still, hands outside his jacket.

Garrett recognized one of them was Harrigan and a thought crossed his mind.

"Gun!" he yelled and dropped instantly into the traditional isosceles shooting stance, arms extended and both hands on his Glock and squeezed off three shots. All struck flesh. All struck one man.

The first tore into Harrigan's right shoulder, shattering bone and a big red stain quickly covered the area. The second was a direct hit to the chest, blowing through the chest bone before lodging in the heart. The third was a superficial hit in his hand.

By the time Harrigan had toppled back into the mud, he was dead.

Standing to the left of the fallen man, Potts, looked down at Harrigan, quickly raised his arms above his head. He dropped his gun into the mud.

– CHAPTER 5 –

AFTER the shooting at the Ranch, Garrett was put on paid leave, surrendered his gun and badge and was told not to come into the office until the administrative investigation board convened in about a week. A union representative met with Garrett several times to prepare him for his appearance.

The day before the board was to meet McBain asked to meet with Chief Morton.

McBain came right out with what was on her mind.

"Garrett shot him purposely," McBain told Morton.

Morton looked sternly at his young bright officer. He had recruited her just for this kind of moment he thought to himself. Now let's see how well she plays in the big time.

"You have been here, what less than a year?" he said. "You understand the gravity of what you are saying here? You are accusing a fellow officer of shooting a man who was attempting to surrender. You know that?"

McBain swallowed hard, stared back at Morton and nodded.

Morton leaned forward on his desk.

"Prove it," he said.

About 10 minutes later McBain finished up. The Chief nodded.

"You got quite a pair on you McBain, you know. I will get you on the witness list for the investigation."

He smiled.

The next day the administrative investigation board comprised of officers from the internal affairs squad in the Sheriff's office in Albany met in a conference room in police headquarters. An audio recording of the proceedings and subsequent transcription preserved the testimony. The board's role was to determine whether Garrett had adhered to the department rule that firearm use of force was legally justified to protect the officer or others from what is reasonably believed to be a threat of death or serious bodily harm.

On the opening day, Garrett was the only witness. He walked the board members through the shooting site behind the Ranch, pointing to where they found a gun on the ground. Then Garrett gave his initial statement in the afternoon.

Garrett explained that there was bad weather and poor visibility that night and he was in a heightened state. He saw a man reach into his pocket and pull out an object. He fired in fear of his life, reminding the board of the gun on the ground.

The men were all standing relatively close to each other and he didn't really aim as much as fire in their direction. The fact that all of his shots squarely hit Harrigan and immediately killed him was just a little bit of bad luck he said.

Garrett felt good about how his account and follow up questioning had gone.

His partner TC, the Medical Examiner, and Chief Morton all testified on the following day. He was not worried about what they might say to the board.

However, on the third and final day of the hearing his mood soured that night when a board member and friend of his from college surreptitiously handed over a transcript of McBain's testimony. As he read it, Garrett got more furious and angry.

High Country Sheriff Office

Administrative Investigation into Death of Albert Harrigan

Day 3

Board: Please state your name and rank.

McBain: Lieutenant Charlotte McBain, High Country Sheriff Office, Company B

Thank you for giving me the opportunity to address the board. My report and conclusion has been made after a careful review of the Medical Examiner's report on the death of Albert Harrigan. Specifically on the bullet that struck Mr. Harrigan in the right hand and not the two bullets that hit him in the chest. This third bullet was given only superficial attention by the ME, as it was not the fatal shots.

Detective Garrett has stated that he thought he saw Harrigan pull out a gun or something from his pocket with his right hand. If you were holding a gun your hand would be closed, clenching the object. (Witness closed her hand).

A bullet hitting that hand would either most likely smash through the fingers and go through the back of the hand or even hit the object, and ricochet who knows where.

However, the ME reports that the bullet was a through and through, passing directly through the palm of Harrigan's hand and out the back. (Witness raises her hand and points to her palm). How could Harrigan have been holding anything in his hand or even looking like he had something in his hand? It couldn't be.

But, if Harrigan had his hands raised like he was surrendering (witness raises her hands above head palms out) a bullet could easily hit his palm and go out the back like the ME reports.

Albert Harrigan wasn't reaching for anything in his pocket or holding anything in his hand that he got from his pocket.

In my opinion Albert Harrigan was surrendering with his hands above his head. Even from where Garrett was and in the dark and rain he could have seen that. Garrett still shot him. He wanted to shoot him.

Thank you

Board: Do you know of any reason why Detective Garrett would shoot Mr. Harrigan if he indeed was giving himself up?

McBain: I can only speculate on a motive. There could have been some personal animosity or history between the two that led the detective to want to shoot him. I don't know much about the Detective's personal life so I would not want to guess what contact if any the Detective had with a man like Harrigan. All I can say is that it looks like from the evidence that Detective Garrett purposely shot Albert Harrigan.

Garrett had read enough and crumpled up the paper, burned it and threw the ashes into the garbage. "That righteous and pompous bitch. Fuck you McBain!"

* * *

The administrative board handed down its ruling a week later. It concluded that it was a justified shooting. In the whirl and chaos of the moment, they found that Garrett had feared for his life when he saw one of the men pull something out of his pocket. The fact that it turned out to be a gun helped support his firing of his gun.

Two days later, Morton called McBain into his office.

"You just learned one of the harsh facts of our job and you need to understand and accept if you are going to do this job well McBain," Morton said, leaning forward, stroking his mustache.

"Stick to your convictions and where the evidence leads you. You are going to be very good at this job. I expect that before you know it you will be running your own department. Now get the hell out of here. I don't want to see you for a few days" he said, motioning with his hand for McBain to get up and leave.

* * *

About two months later, Morton sat in his office looking at the personnel file of Samuel Garrett.

He opened and read through it. Despite the dubious circumstances surrounding the Harrigan shooting, for the most part Garrett had been a good cop with favorable comments. Morton had noted that Garrett's strong investigation skills had helped solve the killing of a family in a botched home invasion and the double homicide of a merchant and his assistant in a jewelry store holdup.

But still Morton had this nagging feeling about Garrett and the gambling rumors. He also sensed that the administrative board decision had raised tensions between McBain and Garrett that permeated inside the squad room.

Morton felt that he had no choice. McBain was staying and Garrett had to go.

A month later, Morton called Garrett into his office and told him that he had arranged a transfer to the Cable Springs department downstate in need of a veteran homicide detective.

Shortly afterwards Garrett packed up his beaten up Toyota with his meager belongings and left.

That was how Garrett found himself sitting in his dumpy apartment in Cable Springs waiting for the next basketball game on TV in a few hours and his next bet.

But he couldn't get rid of the thought on how ironic it was that he had moved more than 200 miles and he still hadn't left his gambling or McBain behind.

– CHAPTER 6 –

SEVERAL miles away from where Hildy sat trembling and alone in the dingy cellar, Cassidy was also alone, slumped in a chair as sunlight streamed into the living room through a big picture window. Hildy was not in the house but still, everywhere he looked he saw her.

There were photos of Hildy– on the big grand piano in the corner, on the wall, over the fireplace and on the glass table. Most were of the two of them smiling, hugging, and kissing from the beaches in Maui to the south of France. They were holding hands in front of Big Ben and the Eiffel Tower and just lounging around the pool in the backyard or in the Palm Springs house.

There were a few photos of Hildy with her younger sister Elsa, who he knew she had been very close to before she had tragically passed away in her teens.

Otherwise, it was Hildy and Cassidy. Almost seven years of good times, no marriage was ever perfect, but for most of the days and nights he was pretty happy.

He reached for the whiskey not sure what to do next. So he sat and drank and remembered where and how he had first met Hildy.

It was a typical soiree during the Christmas holiday high season in the Palm.

Springs desert playground for the rich and famous more than seven years ago. The hostess was Amy Sumner, a wealthy widow and the occasion was the weekend golf tournament named in honor of her late husband at one of the prestigious clubs in the area.

The parking lot was filled with BMWs, Audis, and Porsches. Champagne, wine and cocktails were available at the stand-up bars scattered inside and outside around the pool.

Little black dresses, lightweight wool suits and Hermes ties were the dress of the day. The five-piece and two singers combo filled the room with light rock and dance tune that mingled with the idle banter of the wealthy.

It was a night like so many others for most.

However, for two, it would be an evening that would change their lives forever.

They would joke later that if they had children that they would have been disappointed in hearing how their parents had met.

It wasn't romantic like eyeing each other across the dance floor like Tony and Maria from West Side Story.

It wasn't cute like a set-up date by friends.

No, it started with a bump as he reached in to the shrimp platter and brushed her shoulder.

"I'm so sorry," he said.

She turned around and looked into a Hollywood marquee smile, then blue eyes and immediately felt flush in her face. The next moment she imagined she was looking at Paul Newman.

"Oh my," she blurted out before gaining a bit of composure adding, "no worries. I don't bruise easy."

"I'm RG, but most people call me Cassidy," he said, extending his hand.

Before she could respond, the night's hostess stepped to the lectern on the stage in the front of the room and asked for quiet.

"Friends, I am so glad that you could be here tonight and join us for our weekend festivities, including our golf tournament tomorrow and tonight's gala honoring one of Palm Springs great ladies with this year's Palm Springs Woman of the Year announcement," said Sumner, as there was a round of applause in the room. "A host of wonderful, caring, considerate and giving women who have called Palm Springs their home, have been honored, including First Lady Nancy Reagan, Dolores Hope and Barbara Sinatra. Tonight's honoree stands comfortably with those ladies and all the others we have honored through the decades."

There was a murmur through the crowd, as the name of the honoree was not yet publicly known.

"Before I announce her and ask her to come up to say a few words, let me tell you a little bit about this gracious, loving lady. She is a patron of the arts, supporting our museum and orchestra here as well as back in New York where she lives some of the year.

"This woman is an advocate for so many good causes. She is a leader in the campaign to curb the gun violence that is spreading in our country, especially in our schools. Like others who had stood up here before her, she is a tireless champion of caring for the sick, both here in our area and also back in New York where she and her late husband Charles helped build one of the country's premier departments specializing in infectious diseases in an area hospital. She is truly deserving of this honor and our recognition. I would like to introduce this year's Palm's Springs Woman of the Year and ask her to come on up, Hildy Swanson."

Applause filled the room, and everybody was looking at the two of them.

"I'm Hildy," she said turning to Cassidy with a sheepish grin. "I think they are calling my name."

Cassidy stood with his mouth open. Hildy gave Cassidy her wine glass.

"I'll be back," she said and then added softly, "be here."

Cassidy nodded. "I will."

As Hildy made her way through the room and well-wishers, a woman slid next to him and pointed at Hildy.

"She is a great lady, the best. Hi, my name is Ali," she said extending her hand.

Cassidy turned and saw an elegantly dressed middle-aged woman next to him. She smiled and looked up at Hildy on the stage, who had begun her acceptance speech.

"I've known Hildy for most of my life since we were roommates at Skidmore," said Ali. "She has been one of my dearest friends ever since. Hildy is the most caring person I know. She's helped many of us through hard times."

Ali took a sip of wine and continued, "Hildy has been through some tough times herself. She lost her younger sister Elsa while we were in college. That was hard. So the special hospital wing Elsa's Pavilion for Infectious Diseases is the most important thing in her life."

Hildy had finished and was accepting congratulations as she made her way through the crowd.

"She's a special woman," said Ali, turning and walking away.

Hildy and Cassidy were inseparable the rest of the evening as well-wishers came up to Hildy to congratulate her on the honor. They talked, flirted, and took a few turns around the dance floor. She melted like a teenager in his arms on the dance floor, and tingled with an excitement in her body in places long forgotten when he simply touched her.

He told her about his golf, about being pretty much on his own for years since his parents died and not having much contact with his family. He had been invited by an old college golf teammate to play in the tournament, so he had taken the weekend off from his assistant pro job to come up from Arizona.

She told him about her first marriage of being well provided by her late husband as she spent much of the winter here in Palm Springs before heading back to New York for her other home.

After her husband's sudden passing, Hildy said she had turned to her charitable work and to civic projects ending up with her being honored this evening. Telling Cassidy of her willingness to take a stand on hot-button issues like gun violence and Pro-choice, had led her to become a big fundraiser for numerous politicians who shared her beliefs.

She lived a busy and rewarding life she told Cassidy, but, admitted that she was lonely at times.

They ended the night with a warm embrace and tender kiss; both sensing that there was more to come.

* * *

Cassidy didn't play especially well the next day in the golf event and his team came in third. His friend donated their winnings to a local charity, as was the custom.

That night Hildy and Cassidy slept together. There was no reluctance from either in tumbling into her bed. There was no hesitation from either of them what they wanted from each other.

Cassidy stayed with Hildy the following day, as he had no need to rush back to his job as the club was closed on Mondays.

Their lovemaking was passionate leaving both with the feeling that this was more than just about sex.

"You have stolen my heart Mr. Butch Cassidy," said Hildy, sweetly nuzzling her head into his chest as they lay in bed with the afternoon sunshine filtering through the curtains.

Looking back at that weekend, it felt like a long time ago thought Cassidy.

– CHAPTER 7 –

DR. Stuart Steiner couldn't help but think about Hildy Swanson every time he walked into the gleaming fifth floor atrium of the infectious disease wing at the County Medical Center.

A plaque was prominently placed at the entrance.

Elsa's Pavilion for Infectious Diseases
In Loving Memory from her sister Hildy
Opened May 1998

Nurses and doctors greeted Dr. Steiner with warm hellos and smiles at the unexpected appearance of the department head on a spring Sunday afternoon.

In his office, Dr. Steiner looked at the folder on his desk prepared for tomorrow's board meeting and the notation on his appointment book to meet with Hildy Swanson afterwards. He was hoping to share with her the good news that the board had approved his plan to double the department's budget to continue Hildy's promise of honoring her late younger sister with the finest care possible.

It was more than 20 years ago and several years after her sister Elsa had died of endocarditis when Hildy had come to his office on a cloudy spring day. It was a meeting that would change the trajectory of his life and those of countless future patients.

Dr. Steiner remembered vividly Hildy had said, "You know where I was this morning Dr. Steiner." Without waiting for a reply, she said, "I went to visit Elsa's grave. This is the anniversary of her passing."

Elsa was only a teenager when she came down sick. During the months of treatments, Hildy came home from her senior year in college, never leaving her sister's side during the lengthy ordeal.

"I also drove past King Kone, the ice cream place out on Route 100," said Hildy with a sigh. "Mom and Dad took us there during the summer, we loved going. It was Elsa's favorite. She always got the soft vanilla with sprinkles."

Hildy brushed away a tear.

"I'm sorry," said Dr. Steiner. "She was a good and brave young lady. I am sure that you miss her very much."

Hildy nodded, biting her lower lip to control her emotions. She looked out at the grey sky and wet grounds.

"I think it has rained on every anniversary of her passing," she said. "You know when we were young our Mother told us that when it was raining that God was crying, I think she was right. I do miss her, every single day. You know Doctor when I die I am going to be buried right next to her. That's a promise."

Dr. Steiner nodded.

"So I have another promise, I will also never forget what you did for her and our family. The loving care that you and your staff gave to Elsa and our family while she was here. To keep that promise I would like to create a special wing here at the hospital to study more about these terrible diseases, to come up with cures and to give patients the very best care in the world right here at this hospital. I believe that you Doctor are just the person to develop a comprehensive plan to present to the Board."

"I am honored and somewhat stunned by your proposal," said Dr. Steiner. "I am sure you are aware that building a world-class department to fight and treat these diseases is a huge undertaking."

Hildy nodded.

"And financially?" said Dr. Steiner.

"I have the full support of my husband Charles and we will finance the bulk. Additionally, we put together a series of robust fundraising events. Combined we will have the resources to get it off the ground," said Hildy. "And to sustain it with more than adequate financial support we will set up an endowment fund for as long as we are both alive."

Dr. Steiner smiled and nodded.

"When one of us die the other will continue to financially support the department. Even after I die there will be written into my Will stipulations to continue to fund the department," said Hildy, looking past Dr. Steiner at the gray sky. "That's one more promise."

Now, thinking of the conversation many years later, Dr. Steiner remembered reaching across the desk and shaking Hildy's hand.

Tomorrow, he hoped to have plenty of good news to share with Hildy.

– CHAPTER 8 –

THE estranged son of Hildy's first husband, Gil Swanson was also hoping for good news on Monday, but right now he was sitting down with his old college roommate and his wife for a late Sunday afternoon brunch in a chic midtown New York restaurant forty miles away.

He had one of the best tables in the room where he could be seen and see everybody else. The dining room, bar and outside seating area was filled with a cross-section of New York's well-heeled crowd. Glamorous women were scattered around the room, over in one corner was a Hollywood couple and in another a NBA star sat with his wife. Waiters bustled back and forth with drinks and food orders.

In his early 40's Gil fit into the milieu comfortably with his upper class upbringing, Ivy League education and his impeccable wardrobe that today was "business casual".

Gil liked money and the 5-star hotels, best tables in the finest restaurants, his beachfront house in a gated Miami community and the first class seats that it could buy.

Money and having money was what made Gil get up every morning. On the wall in his Miami penthouse office, he had hung a frame with the words from the Pink Floyd classic, "Money."

Grab that cash with both hands and make a stash.

But lately his stash was shrinking. A messy divorce and some recent failed business ventures could do that.

However, Gil had always felt that his money woes had really started years ago in a midtown conference room sitting across from his stepmother Hildy at the reading of his father Charles' Will.

Gil had been against his father marrying the much younger Hildy right from the start calling her a "gold digger who was only screwing her way into the family fortune."

He hadn't come to the wedding, stayed away from the family for years and didn't attend his father's funeral. But, he was there for the reading of the Will to get what was rightfully his as Charles' only child

"As executor of the Will I think we should get started," had said the lawyer.

"The houses and all possessions including fine art, jewelry and china, all stocks and bonds, saving accounts and car dealership will be given to my wife Hildy," the lawyer read in a firm monotone voice.

Hildy took a noticeable gasp. Gil's mouth dropped and his face turned red.

He angrily pushed back the chair and got up. His face was twisted in anger.

"Nothing! I will get you one day bitch, one day I will get you," he snarled at Hildy as he turned to leave. "One day, bitch!"

Now, sitting in the restaurant with his friends that seemed a long time ago as he raised his wine glass.

"Cheers," said Gil taking a slow sip. "I am so glad that you could free yourself up this afternoon so I could get together with two of my favorite people at one of my favorite places."

"Of course, it's so nice to see you, what's it been almost a year. Luckily, we were able to get somebody to look after the kids," said his old college roommate.

"We know you don't get back that often, so we begged our favorite sitter to come even on a Sunday," said his wife.

"It's a quick trip, got here Friday and out tomorrow night to take care of some business dealings with properties up here and a meeting with my lawyer. How could I not see my old college roommate and his beautiful wife when I am here," said Gil, reaching for a piece of bread.

"It must have been something pretty important for such a quick trip," said the man raising his wine glass. "You look happy. Cheers to a successful conclusion of your business, my friend."

They clicked glasses.

Gil nodded and smiled.

"Plans are already underway to make sure it will be," said Gil.

– CHAPTER 9 –

AT the farmhouse, Bishop guided Hildy through to the back of the kitchen to stairs leading down. The air was damp and musty so she figured she was in a cellar. In her short sleeveless pink dress she felt chilly and vulnerable.

He roughly sat her in a folding chair that was in the middle of the room, took the blindfold off and ripped the tape from her mouth and hands. He didn't tie her up. Where could she go he thought?

"Don't even think about running or screaming, there is nobody within miles of here to help you," he said. "You are here all alone."

Hildy took a big breath to try to calm down and stop from shaking. Bishop took his gun and slowly ran it up her stomach, stopping between her breasts and making a little circle around each of her nipples before pressing the barrel against her mouth.

"I didn't know that you would be such a sexy broad," Bishop said in a soft sinister way.

Hildy clenched her mouth shut. Her nipples hardened and she turned red.

Bishop laughed.

"I am sure you like being alive," he said softly, "We all do. I just wonder what you would do to save your skin. Stand up."

Hesitantly and on trembling legs Hildy stood up. Bishop roughly pulled her to him and tried to kiss her hard on the mouth. But through the rubber mask and small slit for his mouth he couldn't.

"Shit!" he said.

Bishop stepped back and pushed up the mask. He yanked Hildy to him and pressed his mouth on her, but Hildy kept her mouth closed shut. He angrily pulled back and ripped off the top button on her dress. Then the second and all of them until the dress hung open to her stomach.

Hildy was breathing heavily. Bishop too took a deep breath letting his eyes run up and down her.

Hildy steeled herself for what was likely to happen next. She looked intently at her attacker.

He had a weathered face from being outside, with a strong jaw and chin with a thick light brown mustache. His mouth was curled in an evil grin and his eyes were cold and hard.

The touch of hard steel sent shivers through Hildy as Bishop again ran the barrel of his gun lightly down her chest to her stomach.

Hildy took another deep breath and remembered a time many years ago when a date night turned into a date rape and how she had fought the man off with her nails and even her teeth. She would do it again with this animal she thought.

Bishop took a step closer, but suddenly she raised her hands and clawed at his neck with her sharp nails. Her nails dug into open skin and quickly blood seeped out of long ugly wounds on both sides of his neck.

"Bitch!" he said, stepping back in a bit of shock. He felt the blood on both sides of his neck and wiped the left side with his hand. Bishop looked down at the blood on his on his hand.

Bishop raised his hand ready to slap her when the door behind him swung open.

"Hey! We don't need that shit right now," Thornton yelled as he marched into the room, his mask still on. "Pull your goddam mask down."

"She cut me!" snarled Bishop, as he struggled to get his mask back on. "Bitch! I am going to …"

"You're not going to do anything right now," said Thornton moving closer. "We are going to stick to the plan."

Bishop stared at Hildy. He grinned slightly, wiped his hand on the shoulder of her dress, and then abruptly ripped off a piece and flung it on the floor.

"Plenty of time for your ass later," Bishop said.

He turned, and followed by Thornton walked out, closing the door with a thud.

Hildy sat like a scared little school child, her feet and legs tightly crossed, wrapping her arms around her body to keep her tattered dress from completely falling off.

She took a deep breath and tried to let the tension out of her body. She looked around. She was in a basement, no lights, cement walls, two small windows high on one wall letting in some sunlight. A rust-stained sink was against one wall, a dirty mattress and a pile of dirt and debris stacked up against the far wall.

There was no way out, she was alone and trapped.

Upstairs, Thornton slammed the cellar door shut, put the lock on it and followed Bishop up the stairs. In the kitchen Thornton angrily yanked off his mask and sat down.

"Why you need to pull that crap with her," he snapped "Just fucking keep it in your pants just once, OK?"

Bishop went over to a cooler on the floor in the corner, pulled out a beer, opened it, making sure to flip the top with his fingerprints back into the cooler and sat down. He took a big drink. There was a bottle of Jack Daniels on the table with a couple of paper cups.

"Why not," he said. "I would have given you some. That's a hot piece of tail there, just sitting there for us to enjoy while we can."

Thornton shook his head and poured a shot into a cup.

"You just think with one head," he said. "You fuck her and your cum would have been all over her or in her. And that means your goddam DNA."

Bishop smiled and pulled out a pack of Trojans from his pants pocket.

Thornton shook his head and frowned. "Still stupid."

The two looked at each other. Outside the light was beginning to fade.

Neither man talked. They could hear a flock of birds chirping in a nearby tree.

Bishop wiped some of the blood off his neck with his hand and tore off a sheet of paper towel lying on the table and dabbed at the deep scratch.

"Damn that bitch!" he said.

Thornton looked at him and shrugged his shoulders. "Your own fucking fault…"

Now Bishop shrugged his shoulders, taking the paper towel off the scratch and carefully placing it in a plastic bag of garbage next to the table.

Thornton took a long gulp of beer.

"Now we just wait and follow the plan," he said.

– CHAPTER 10 –

HILDY too was waiting for something to happen, but she didn't know what.

Once the two men had left, she had gotten up from the chair to look around her grimy prison. There was not much to see or find. No hammer or big piece of wood she could even think about using against her kidnappers. She tried to peer out the windows but even on her tippy-toes she was not able to reach. All she knew that it was getting dark outside.

She had no idea where she was. Who was holding her? Why and what they were going to do with or to her.

She slumped back in the chair, pulling her ripped dress around her tightly. She continued to tremble. And wait.

* * *

Several miles away and a few hours later, the doorbell rang and Cassidy checked his iPhone – 7:45. It would be his business colleague and friend Tyree Harris. On Friday he had invited him over to watch the Sunday night basketball game with him. Cassidy had decided to keep the evening's plans to maintain normal appearances despite the kidnapping of his wife.

"Need to keep my cool, Showtime," whispered Cassidy as he opened the door.

As Tyree entered the foyer Cassidy slapped him on his back and said, "Let's go get some beers T. The game is going to start soon."

As the two settled into their chairs, beers in hands to watch the game on the big screen TV, Cassidy turned to Tyree.

"Tomorrow I won't be in," Cassidy said of his job as the General Manager at the local car dealership owned by his wife. "Got some personal business to take care of."

Tyree nodded.

"No problem, boss, not much going on tomorrow anyway," he said. "Hope nothing serious."

"Just a few things I need to do," said Cassidy.

Tyree looked around the room as he took a large swallow.

"Where's Hildy," he said.

Cassidy took a moment.

"She's out for a while," he said.

* * *

Out at the darkened farmhouse, Bishop looked at his watch.

"It's time," he said.

He finished off the Jack Daniels with a gulp, put down the glass, and got up. Only a small candle in the middle of the table shed any light in the room. Bishop turned on the flashlight and shined it in Thornton's face.

"Let's go," he said.

Both picked up their guns, slipped them into their waistbands and put on their gloves. They went to the basement door.

"This time we do it right," Bishop said grimly as he unlocked and opened the cellar door.

Hildy tensed up as a beam of light came down the stairs, followed by the two men. She clutched her hands and crossed her legs tightly. Hildy watched them come across the room until they stood just a few feet from her.

She could see guns in their waistbands.

Hildy noticed something different.

The men were not wearing their masks.

– CHAPTER 11 –

HILDY called it the Trophy Room.

After Tyree had left around 11:00 at the end of the game, Cassidy tried to sleep but after an hour of tossing and turning he gave up. He got up, grabbed a beer from the refrigerator and walked into the Trophy Room to plop down wearily in the desk chair and turn on the desk light.

Cassidy looked around the small room off the main living area. Hildy had filled it with photos, trophies, and even old scrapbooks full of news clippings of Cassidy's golf accomplishments.

Cassidy grew up playing golf from an early age like the rest of the family. His father Lee, a 10-handicap player, taught all of the kids the game, managing to find time on weekends or after work as a sales clerk at the nearby Home Depot. Quickly it became apparent that Cassidy showed the most talent and interest in the game and Lee began to lavish most of his attention on him.

On the wall behind the desk, Hildy had framed two San Diego Union Tribune stories. Cassidy took them both down.

Local Golfer Wins State Junior Crown

RG Cassidy of Lemon Grove is 14 and under state champion

The other heralded his getting a golf scholarship to perennial college powerhouse Oklahoma State.

RG Cassidy's Golf Career Headed to Big Time Oklahoma State

He put the frames back on the wall and picked up a photo on the desk.

It was his favorite memory showing him with his Dad hugging each other off the 18th green at Laughlin's Fields on the final day of Qualifying School for the Nationwide Tour 12 years ago.

He smiled. He had been a winner that day!

That had been the best day of his golfing life. On his first try he had qualified for what was then called the Nationwide Tour, the stepping-stone to the lush purses and green fairways of the PGA Tour. Only big things waited for him he had thought that sticky Florida afternoon.

Making that day even more special was that he had beaten his rival from the juniors and college Ace Hammond for the last qualifying spot.

Paired together for the final round, Cassidy remembered coming to the perilous 18th hole clinging to a 1-shot lead and thinking that a par 4 would likely be enough for him to win.

After both hit good drives, Cassidy's second shot into the elevated green was short and rolled back into a deep swale. Ace put his second shot safely on the green.

Cassidy could still feel how dry his mouth and sweaty his palms were, as he got ready to hit his third shot.

Cassidy never remembered exactly what happened next. He didn't see the ball softly hit just on the fringe of the green and then roll and roll straight into the hole for the most unlikely and amazing birdie he had ever made.

Cassidy looked over at Ace who stood stunned and ashen. He had watched in horror as his hopes dropped into the cup.

Rattled, Ace badly missed his birdie putt and barely made the par putt to end two shots behind Cassidy and out of the last qualifying spot. Ace stormed off the green without a word while Cassidy's Dad and others came out to hug and congratulate him.

It was only later in the locker room that Ace said something that stayed with Cassidy ever since.

"You are the luckiest son of a bitch in the world," Ace snarled, jabbing his finger at Cassidy. "One of these days you are going to run out of luck. You just watch out! One of these days you will get yours."

To this day Cassidy was still haunted by the venom and anger of Ace's threat as he had stormed out of the locker room. Ace never made it to the Nationwide Tour and the last Cassidy heard he was an assistant pro somewhere in Texas.

In the Texas heat that night, a naked woman rested on her hands and knees on the disheveled bed in the sparsely furnished house. She peered over her shoulder at the naked man standing on the side of the bed and smiled.

"Harder. Do it again harder," she cooed, grinning.

Ace looked at the woman. Her creamy white ass stood out in contrast to the bronzed legs and back that was only marred by tiny bathing suit lines from hours of lounging around the pool in the hot sun.

Her ass was splotched red from where he had already spanked her.

She was one of those bored housewives from Dallas or Houston who came for a girls' getaway. They came they said to play a little golf or tennis, to hang around at the resort pool and bar. What they really were doing was getting away from their rich husbands and nagging kids to put some fun back into their lives and beds.

Ace couldn't remember her name. Missy or Melissa? Yes, it was Melissa. He had gone over to her at a town bar popular with resort guests to ask her to dance to Sweet Melissa from the Allman Brothers and conversation was immediately started as she said that was her name.

The evening quickly progressed from dances, drinks to her following him to his place to shedding clothes even before they got to the bedroom. Now she was on all fours, naked, peering over her shoulder, smiling, wanting it harder, again.

He moved behind her. She wanted it harder; he would give it to her harder.

An hour later Ace sat naked on his couch. She was still on the bed, sleeping. Like many nights the sex was good and plentiful for him. It was about the only thing good and plentiful in this lousy place he thought taking a gulp of beer.

He was only an assistant pro at a small private course a little out of town. It was pretty much a dead end job Ace knew, but when he spun his story with a little exaggeration of almost reaching the PGA Tour the women were impressed. It also helped that he was a strapping 6 foot-3inches.

Ace took another long gulp. The beer was still cold, about the only thing that stayed cold in the springtime heat here he said to himself. How had he come to living here in this worn down house on the outskirts of town, in this place with little future to be excited about, except for the next woman he would bring home? He shot a glance into the bedroom where Melissa had begun to stir.

This was his pitiful little life he thought. What had happened to all of those dreams of fame and fortune he had?

But, Ace knew exactly how his life had fallen into disarray. The events of that afternoon in the sticky Florida sunshine and humidity were burned into his mind night and day. He woke up remembering and went to sleep dreaming about it. Never would he come that close again to qualifying for the Nationwide Tour.

Tonight, though, he felt like that weight had been lifted off his shoulders. He had stopped waiting for something good to happen and with the assistance of two college buddies had recently put into action steps to turn his life around. He smiled and he wondered how things were going a thousand miles away? Tomorrow would be the big day as he took a long swig of beer.

He put the bottle down on the table and looked at the folder on the table filled with papers. A color brochure was on top. He picked it up and smiled.

"Trencher's Farm," he said. "I like the way that sounds."

* * *

In the Trophy Room Cassidy got up from his chair and in the semi darkness with his drink in his hand he wandered around the room. As he looked at the photos on the walls and the trophies in the case, a pall fell around him. Despite the headlines, happy photos and trophies and medals displayed in the room, Cassidy knew that in reality he had been a loser on the golf course.

His brief stay on the Nationwide Tour was marked by a lot of missed cuts and small paydays, but probably the most disappointing day of his golf career was when he was a senior at Oklahoma and had a chance to win the NCAA title for the Sooners with a birdie on the last hole of his match.

But, when he dumped his third shot into the sand on the par-5 closing hole so too sank Oklahoma's chances of winning.

That night on the long trip back from Arizona to Norman Cassidy remembered sitting alone, staring blankly out the window and thinking he was a loser.

But tonight, sitting alone again with darkness all around him again, Cassidy felt something different.

As he dozed off in the chair, surrounded by photos of trophies of happy days yet haunted by his failures, he had one final thought.

He just knew he would be a winner tomorrow!

– CHAPTER 12 –

THE cold water jolted the life back into Cassidy as he stood under the shower nozzle on full blast.

He had managed to doze off a little in the chair while he was in the Trophy Room, but it was not a restful sleep. He woke up Monday morning stiff in the joints and groggy and had hurried off to the shower. Today was going to be a big day and Cassidy knew he had to be mentally and physically alert to be a winner.

Last night Cassidy had worked out that the best way to get the $300,000 in cash the kidnappers had demanded without raising suspicion was to take it out of the car dealership business account at the bank.

So, Cassidy walked into the bank on Cable Springs' main street when it opened promptly at 9:00. He had carefully dressed in business attire and carried a leather briefcase. The bank was the biggest in town with a commercial division and was a branch of a national group. Both the business and Hildy's and Cassidy's joint personal accounts had been held at the bank for years.

Many times Cassidy had dealt with the bank manager on regular business transactions but he still always felt a bit uneasy around the man. Cassidy thought that the middle-aged man patronized him, talking down to him, using complicated banking language to explain matters. When Hildy came into the office, however, the manager treated her like royalty, offering her coffee or tea and even a plate of cookies.

Now Cassidy fidgeted in his chair sitting across from the manger in his office.

"This is very irregular, sir," said the bank manager, adjusting his glasses nervously. "Your normal business withdrawals are around $10,000. Today it is $300,000. That's a lot of cash."

Cassidy had rehearsed his explanation. He nodded and leaned forward in his chair.

"We have an unexpected expense at the dealership and need cash today," he said. "A larger than usual shipment of high-end, pre-owned cars is available immediately to build up our summer inventory. The summer months are usually our busiest, you know."

"I see," said the manager.

"The bank can handle it?" Cassidy said.

"Oh, yes sir. You have more than enough in the business account to cover it and we have that amount of cash available in our vault," the manager said quickly. "It will just take a few minutes to fill out the paperwork and get the cash together. We might have to give you smaller bills."

Cassidy nodded.

"Hundreds, fifties and even twenties are good, as long as it has Uncle Sam's signature on it," he said with a smile. "I just need the money now. I have an important appointment later."

Forty-five minutes later Cassidy walked out into the brilliant sunshine carrying the briefcase in his right hand. Inside in neatly wrapped stacks in rubber bands was $300,000.

– CHAPTER 13 –

"YOU look like shit, Detective," said the big man sliding onto the counter stool next to him in the diner.

The diner, directly across from the bank on the main street in town, was packed for Monday morning breakfast on another nice spring day. The sun was out in a blue sky sprinkled with a few white clouds. It looked like a great start to for most of the people in Cable Springs.

Detective Garrett was not one of the many. He turned to the man on the stool. It was Rudy. He was a big man, big arms, big chest, big hands and big mustache. Not fleshy, but big as in big and strong. And mean and rough.

Rudy hurt people. He had even killed people. .

Usually Rudy didn't want to be seen with him in very public spaces and met at night in a dumpy little roadhouse bar up county off Route 22 thought Garrett. What was this about he wondered as he stirred his coffee?

"Coffee" Rudy said to the waitress.

Garrett looked down at his black coffee.

"Tough night again for you? What, you have the Hawks plus the Lakers? Shit." Rudy said shaking his head.

Garrett kept on staring down at his coffee. He had USA Today opened to the NBA page on the counter.

Rudy looked at the paper and shook his head.

"Shit, you are going to do it again tonight aren't you," he said. "Basketball is a sucker bet. When you going to realize that? I hope soon, because the man says you are now in for us for 15 grand. That's not good."

Garrett kept on staring down at his coffee.

"You, my friend have a few problems. One, you bet a lot, probably more than you should or can afford on what you make as one of our local finest. Second, you are a lousy bettor. You lose a lot. You are always picking losers. That's not a good combination."

The waitress brought Rudy his coffee. He took a sip and kept talking in a low ominous tone.

"We know of your issues in the High Country. We knew Harrigan. Did some business with him. Not a nice guy so we didn't shed any tears after what happened. What you say in the inquest, that it was a lucky shot that you hit him, not the other guy with the gun?"

Rudy chuckled and took a sip of his coffee.

"Yeah, lucky shot my ass. You saw your chance and you took it. That showed a lot of balls, or a lot of desperation. We knew all that but were willing to take a chance and give you a shot. We like to support our local police department."

At that Rudy grinned and continued, "But, how you got out of your debt up there is not going to happen down here. We operate a little bit different down here. I make sure of that, that's my job."

Rudy turned and gripped Garrett's arm. He pulled back his sports jacket to show a gun packed in his waistband.

He took another sip of his coffee, put his massive forearms on the table and turned and edged close to Garrett.

"We are going to give you two ways of clearing up your debt, Detective," said Rudy in a threatening whisper. "As you can imagine with all of our enterprises going on, it would be very helpful to have somebody inside the police department giving us a heads up on any investigations or raids. Our eyes and ears. Our snitch."

Garrett blinked his eyes and swallowed hard.

In his heart, Garrett thought of himself as a good cop. He had a clean record, kept that way when the Board had found him innocent of any wrong doing in the shooting of Harrigan. Garrett knew of his true intentions in the High Country, but he could live with that.

He wasn't a great cop, just a cop. He didn't let his partner out to dry, didn't turn his eye on matters and did his job. Those were words of advice his Uncle John gave him at the time he had joined the force, and he lived up to that standard. If his uncle were still alive he would be fine with his record and pleased to have the tradition of having a cop in the family continued.

But, like most people Garrett was a flawed person. Some drank too much. Some cheated on their spouses. Some lied on their tax returns. He bet too much and recently he couldn't pick a winner.

But, being asked to turn informant for the local Mob made him more than simply a flawed person. It would make him a dirty cop. He could just imagine his uncle turning over in his grave if he did that.

"If you do that, we would forgive the 15 grand," said a grinning Rudy, snapping Garrett back to the present. "If you can't stomach that Detective, there is a second option,

"We give you thirty days to pay back the whole 15 grand. Thirty days. After thirty days, I come for you again and this time we won't be meeting out in public before all of these fine people. You understand?"

Rudy stood up.

"Oh, we are cutting you off starting now," Rudy said balling up the newspaper and tossing it into the garbage can behind the counter. "No more bets. You got a couple of days to think about our offer, or start pulling the money together. It's your choice, your life. I will be seeing you soon. Thirty days."

Rudy walked out.

Garrett absent-mindedly stirred his coffee as he stirred things in his mind.

"Fuck."

– CHAPTER 14 –

DR. STEINER was despondent.

He had gone into the Monday morning budget meeting confident his proposed funding increase would be met. Through tireless effort he and his staff had built his infectious disease department into one of the national leaders in the field. In prestige alone his department had raised the prominence of the hospital. Long in the shadow of the huge institutions and prominent names of the New York City hospitals, Dr. Steiner's work had helped the hospital become recognized on its own and attract new corporate partners and generous donors.

But, Dr. Steiner was not satisfied. For the Board, he had outlined an ambitious expansion of the department in the coming fiscal year.

He had expected that there would be a little push back on the proposed budget. So he had included a few line items he would be ready to cut as part of his negotiating strategy. Dr. Steiner had it all figured out.

So he never expected to hear that because of setbacks in other departments and a slight decrease in patients, that there would be no increase in his budget and possibly even a 20 percent cut. This would effectively shelve his plans to expand and modernize his department.

Dr. Steiner left the meeting enraged, his temper only soothed a little by the sense of pride and satisfaction he always got when he walked past the Elsa's Pavilion sign on the wall heading into the sunlight filled airy atrium that immediately lifted visitors and patient spirits. This was the centerpiece of his unit that occupied an entire corner of the hospital's second floor. The department had a dozen spacious single occupancy patient rooms, a large lab with the most up-to-date equipment in the field, and several consultation rooms.

He had an exceptional staff of nurses, researchers and some of the best medical school grads in the field.

Now as he walked past the reception desk and waiting area to his office he seethed with frustration.

There was one option that still was available. He was a little reluctant to use it as he never wanted to take advantage of it, but in this case he felt he really had no alternative.

He looked at the clock. 11:00 a.m.

Last week, in advance of what he thought would be a successful Board meeting and the good news that he was expecting to share, he had set up an appointment with Hildy Swanson for this morning. Now it would be for him to share the bad news.

"Margaret, has anybody seen Hildy," he said to his secretary as he walked into his office.

He leaned back in his chair and thought of all of the hard work and big plans he had that were now suddenly in doubt. Then he thought about Hildy and managed a small smile.

Hildy had always promised to be there to help.

"Margaret! Is Hildy here yet?" he said.

– CHAPTER 15 –

ACCORDING to the official rules of golf there can be 14 clubs in a player's bag.

Rarely or ever is a player packing a Smith and Wesson 39 semi-automatic pistol in his golf bag.

Cassidy had changed into his golf clothes when he got back from the bank. It was now a little before noon and he squatted before a small safe in the back of the bedroom closet that was open. Cassidy reached in and pulled out a gun. He had gotten the gun and license several years ago when there had been a series of house break-ins around the area. Hildy thought they should have one. They also put in a start-of-the-art alarm and surveillance system. The robbery gang had been caught several months into its crime spree and the gun stayed tucked away in the safe until now.

Cassidy picked up the gun and walked out of the bedroom to the garage. He got his golf bag and slipped the gun in the side pocket. He placed the briefcase with the $300,000 on the car seat next to him and drove out.

At the end of the driveway, he turned left and headed toward the Trencher's Farm golf course. It was about a half hour drive to the course.

At a red light, Cassidy's cell phone rang. He looked down. It was Tyree. Cassidy frowned.

"Hello," he said guardedly.

"Cassidy, lot of fun last night, always nice hanging out with you," Tyree said cheerfully. "Just checking in with you on this beautiful spring day. I got a feeling you are heading to a tennis court or some other fun activity today instead of being here in this damn office. Personal business my ass! Wish I was with you."

Cassidy swallowed.

"I wish T,' he said slowly.

Cassidy took another breath and then told him what was happening.

"Oh, shit Cassidy, you should have told me last night so we could have made plans. You gotta call the cops," said Tyree.

"I can't," said Cassidy as he pulled to a stop at another red light. "They told me no cops. If they found out I did that, I think they would kill Hildy."

There was a moment's silence.

"I guess so, but you can't do this alone. Let me come, where are you going? I can watch from a distance, they would never see me," said Tyree. " I could take down their license plate, you know get a description of them for the cops afterwards. You know be a witness for you."

The light turned green.

"I can't take that chance, it's too risky," Cassidy said.

There was more silence as Cassidy made a turn onto the road where the club was located.

"I have a gun," he said.

"What? You have a gun with you! Fuck, I didn't even know you had a gun," said Tyree.

Cassidy told him about getting the gun several years ago and putting it in his golf bag.

Cassidy slowed at the entrance to Trencher's Farm.

"I think I could use it if have the chance," Cassidy said. "T, I think I really could kill these scumbags."

– CHAPTER 16 –

DRIVING up the long tree lined driveway to the stately white-faced clubhouse, Cassidy knew from the website and taking a virtual tour of the Trencher's Farm course that the immaculate looking fairway and manicured green on his left was the 9th hole.

The parking lot was about half full. Cassidy didn't see anybody else as he took out his bag and put on his shoes.

Opened in 1991, Trencher's Farm was named after the owner of the property Ben Trencher.

A relatively newcomer on the Westchester County golf scene as compared to historic clubs like Winged Foot and Westchester Country Club, Trencher's Farms had quickly established itself as one of the premier courses in the area as annually ranked by Westchester Monthly.

The par 71, 7,100-yard course was an Eli David design and was described on the website as "tucked into a picturesque landscape of rolling hills, meandering creeks and streams, and forests." It offered a traditional layout of 11 par-4s, 4 par-3s and 3-par 5s.

While he had been on the website he had noticed on the Pro Shop and Club Professional staff page a Help Wanted

75

announcement for an assistant pro and head of golf programs position. Cassidy figured that at a club like Trencher's Farm it probably paid well with a nice base salary and commission on all lessons and programs.

Cassidy smiled. Maybe a few years ago he would have been interested in pursuing such a nice money making opportunity. But, not anymore he thought. He didn't have to pursue any opportunities.

He carefully locked the car, putting the briefcase with the money in the trunk, and with his golf bag slung over his shoulder walked into the pro shop.

"I'm Mr. Cassidy. I'm in the 1 o'clock tee time," said Cassidy to the young lady behind the counter.

"Yes, Mr. Cassidy, we have a threesome under your name booked at 1 o'clock," she said. "The other members Mr. Bishop and Mr. Thornton have not checked in yet. Will you be paying for all three and carts?"

Cassidy frowned and nodded.

"Once your group is all here you can immediately go off," she said handing Cassidy a receipt and his credit card. "We have a charity event starting at 4:30 today with a shotgun start on all 18 holes so you are the last group off. In fact the 12:50 group never showed so you should have clear playing all the way around. Enjoy."

Cassidy walked out, put his bag into a cart and drove over to the 1st tee.

As he stood there limbering up Cassidy soaked in the sunshine and comfortable mid-70s temperatures as he looked out at the fairway. An ideal day for a round of golf, just like so many others ones he had played before thought Cassidy. So, why then was his mouth so dry and his hands so clammy?

At exactly 1:00 two men drove up in a cart. They got out and walked over to Cassidy.

"I'm Bishop," said the taller of the two as he took his clubs and put them in Cassidy's cart. "This is Thornton."

Both had hats pulled down low and were dressed in standard golf attire.

The starter looked at the three men.

"I see only two sets of clubs, one of you is not playing?" he said.

"Our friend is just learning the game and only watching," said Bishop motioning with his head at Thornton. "Don't worry we paid for three rounds."

The starter shrugged his shoulders.

"Doesn't make any difference. If you are ready the tee is yours. Enjoy," he said as he headed back to the pro shop.

Bishop slid into the cart next to Cassidy. Thornton walked over to Cassidy's side and pulled up his shirt a little exposing a butt of a gun stuck in his waistband.

"Just to remind you, in case you want to cause any trouble," said Bishop. "It's going to be match play, win or lose the hole, final score of the round doesn't matter. But, with one little twist to our game for you to win."

Then Bishop grinned and said, "It's called Hangman."

One of his elementary school teachers had introduced him and his class to the game as a way to make spelling fun. The teacher had said the game went all the way back to England in the 17th century when prisoners facing death demanded the "Rite of Words and Rites."

It was a fancy title for a simple game. The prisoner had the opportunity to guess a word and if they were right, they would be allowed to live. If they didn't, they were executed. Nowadays the popular game had evolved into one played with pen and pencil.

Thornton handed Bishop a clipboard with a piece of paper and sharpie.

"You have to win a game of Hangman," said Bishop.

On the paper was a crude sketch of the Hangman scaffold (writer's note – here I would add a sketch of the hangman)

"There are six parts of the Hangman, head, body, two arms, two legs," said

Bishop. "It's pretty simple. We have just updated it for our golf game. For every hole you lose, I draw another part of the body. For every hole we halve (tie) or you win nothing, and you take another hole off the board. Again pretty simple, you lose six holes, it's over."

Cassidy nodded.

The two walked up to the first tee.

"Strict Rules of Golf?" said Bishop.

"Of course."

– CHAPTER 17 –

AS they stood on the 9th hole tee and looked out at the rather benign par-4 called the Straight Shooter, Cassidy was frustrated. As he feared, his game was rusty. Years ago, the only game he played was golf. Now, he spent his Sundays on the tennis court and not the golf course.

He had lost three of the first eight holes and the Hangman was beginning to swing with a head, body and one arm.

Reflecting on the opening holes, Cassidy was both upset with his own poor play and the unbelievably lucky shot Bishop hit on the third hole that started a streak of him losing three consecutive holes.

On the par-5 third called the Gambler, Bishop had miraculously holed out with a fairway wood with his second shot for a double eagle.

One hole lost.

Cassidy had mishit the tee shot on the next hole with a drive far into the woods on the par-4 that was appropriately called Redwoods. He easily lost that hole.

Two holes lost.

Still looking for his game, Cassidy had plopped his tee shot into one of the many bunkers surrounding the par-3 fifth hole called Sahara to lose that hole.

Three holes lost.

They halved the next two holes and Cassidy even managed to win the 8th hole with a par.

But then things really got interesting riding up the 9th fairway.

"Fuck," said Bishop slamming on the brakes of the cart some 15 yards short of where both balls lay in the middle of the fairway.

Cassidy saw the same thing.

Behind the 9th green, parked outside the clubhouse entrance were two State police cars. Two cops were standing next to their car, one of them cradling a shotgun.

"Cops!" said Bishop turning to Cassidy. "What are they doing here?"

Cassidy shook his head.

Thornton pulled up alongside. He had a worried look on his face and shot anxious glances at both men.

They sat in their carts in the middle of the fairway waiting and watching.

"Well, we can't just sit here," Cassidy finally said. "That would bring more attention to us."

Bishop quickly nodded and drove up to their balls that were about 10 yards apart.

Both Cassidy and Bishop nervously missed their shots into a greenside sand trap.

They drove slowly up to the green and both hurriedly blasted out of the bunker.

A moment later the clubhouse front door swung open. Two more uniformed State policemen walked quickly out to their car escorting a member of the grounds crew, dressed in overalls and tee shirt, between the two. His hands were clasped at his waist. As he got closer, Cassidy could see that he was handcuffed.

The two cops got the prisoner into their car and climbed in.

"You're away Cassidy," said Bishop marking his ball on the green.

Officer Longtree lowered the shotgun and opened the car door. He stopped and looked toward the three men on to the green, who were not more than 30 yards away. Bishop and Thornton had pulled their hats down almost over their eyes to cover their faces.

"Wish I was out there with you. Looks like a great day for a round. Have a good game," Officer Longtree shouted over, eyeing them intently.

"Yeah, a beautiful day to play Officer," said Cassidy, with a little wave.

"Come on Longtree," said his partner Officer Johnson, who was already inside their car. "Let's get going and let them enjoy the game. You don't even play golf."

Longtree tipped his cap and slid into the front seat.

The two cop cars pulled away and down the driveway.

Standing on the green, Bishop, Cassidy and Thornton looked at each other; eyes wide open and took deep breaths.

"That was close," said Thornton.

"Yeah, " said Cassidy. "Let's get going."

Bishop and Cassidy tied the hole and quickly got over to the 10th tee.

– CHAPTER 18 –

AS the TV announcers like to say, in big golf tournaments, the back nine on Sunday afternoons is what separates the winners and losers. As he climbed out of the cart at the 10th tee, Cassidy remembered feeling that kind of pressure when he had been playing tournament golf. Then he had welcomed the challenge of trying to play his best golf in crunch time and he would have to do the same now he thought.

One thing was for sure - the arithmetic was pretty simple. He could not lose another three holes, or the Hangman would have a full body.

Cassidy's mood brightened when he took the next three holes off the board by halving the 10th and 12th and winning the 11th.

The odds were now a bit more favorable Cassidy thought. There were six holes left to play and all he had to do was win or tie four of them. Bishop drove up to the 13th tee of the par-5 called Cripple Creek for the stream that protected the green.

But it was unlucky 13 for Cassidy.

Both Cassidy and Bishop hit good tee shots. On his second shot a confident Cassidy went for the green.

From about 220 yards out and in the middle of the fairway, Cassidy took a good and mighty swing and the ball climbed through the sky high and straight. But it was not a good enough swing.

The ball ran out of speed and fell into the water with a splash.

Now hitting his fourth shot after taking a stroke penalty, Cassidy managed to get within 10 feet of the hole.

But it didn't save the hole. Bishop won it with a birdie putt, after playing more conservatively on his second shot and lofting a crisp wedge to within six feet of the pin.

The Hangman now had its' head, body, two arms, and was missing just the two legs.

There were five holes to go.

– CHAPTER 19 –

STRIDING up to the tee on the 14th Cassidy saw the man first.

He was a member of the grounds crew, cleaning up some debris and raking the fairway bunker on the left side of the par-4 dogleg called Across the Great Divide that featured a deep gully in front of an elevated green.

Bishop and Thornton's plan was to stay incognito as much as possible for the round and so far it had gone as hoped. They had not seen anybody on the course until the encounter with the cops on the 9th green and now.

But here was this man who would certainly get a decent view of them when they got down to the bend in the fairway.

Thornton joined Cassidy and Bishop on the tee. They stared at the man for several moments. Then the three looked at each other.

"Well, let's do it," said Cassidy as he teed up his ball and the others nodded.

Standing outside the bunker leaning on his rake, Geno too was eyeing the men carefully as he thought there was something a little odd with this threesome on the tee.

There were two carts but only two sets of clubs in one cart and that was always a bit unusual. He squinted his eyes to get a little bit better view. At times like this, he wished that he had listened to his wife and gotten those glasses he needed.

His weather beaten face wrinkled up in a bit of a frown and he rubbed his black mustache in a nervous habit as he waved to signal that he was watching and that they could hit away.

Cassidy played the safe tee shot, putting the ball into the middle of the fairway right at the bend. Bishop took a more aggressive approach by looking to cut the dogleg.

Geno heard the solid sound of a well-struck shot. The ball flew majestically toward the bend.

But, watching, Geno knew right away that the shot didn't have a chance. Rarely was somebody able to cut the corner he knew from all of his years at the club.

The ball started fading to the right. Geno nodded.

Geno heard Bishop plead, "Stay up, stay up," leaning to his left to keep the ball from crashing into the woods. Deep into the woods it went and out of sight. Bishop angrily picked up his tee.

Geno chuckled and shook his head as he watched two of the group get into a cart and drive down the fairway. The third man stayed behind and walked to the port-a-john just off the tee.

"Damn," Bishop said loudly as he jumped out of the cart next to the woods where his ball had sailed in.

Bishop stormed into the thick woods.

Cassidy got out of the cart. He looked back up the fairway and didn't see Thornton in his cart. He casually went to his bag, noticing that Geno was staring at them.

Cassidy pulled out the Smith & Wesson and covering it with his hand chambered a round. He held the gun at his side. He followed Bishop into the woods.

Cassidy found Bishop kicking the brush with his foot looking for the ball. Bishop looked up at Cassidy.

* * *

Later Geno would tell the police that he really couldn't describe the men, that they were across the fairway and that he wished that he had gotten those glasses his wife had been nagging him about for months. He could say that he saw two of them go into the woods first and heard voices and what sounded like an argument.

Geno remembered hearing one say "Hildy," and "police," and point something at the other.

That's when the third man drove up and walked into the woods. After a few minutes all three walked out and back into their carts to finish the hole. Geno thought he saw the third man put a black object into his golf bag.

Geno said he was sorry that he couldn't help more except to say that the threesome was a "bit odd and hard to forget".

– CHAPTER 20 –

"KILLER of a hole, huh," said Bishop standing on the 16th hole tee looking out at the large expanse of water that twinkled in the sunlight.

Cassidy looked out to the small peninsula green on the course's signature hole, the par-3 called Lifeboat.

A short hole it had a big reputation as one of the top 18 holes in Westchester County in the yearly ratings by Westchester Monthly. It was one of four par-3s on the list along with the 7th hole at Old Oaks, the 10th at Mount Kisco CC and the 17th at Summit Club.

"I'm sure that it's been a watery grave for many," Bishop said smiling as he turned to look directly at Cassidy. Thornton chuckled.

Cassidy too smiled. He had a more relaxed air about him now. He had won the 14th, halved the 15th. There were just three holes left and Bishop still needed to win two, finally giving Cassidy a little wiggle room.

However, there wasn't much room for a mistake on this hole. The tee shot was a direct carry over water to the green. Off to a corner of the pond was the namesake lifeboat moored complete with a golfer mannequin holding a fishing line. Cute thought Cassidy. Maybe he was looking for all of the balls or possibly other objects that must rest at the bottom of the water.

No time to dwell on the water Cassidy said to himself as he prepared to hit his tee shot.

Cassidy caught his tee shot just a little on the heel of his 9-iron. It came off low.

Cassidy leaned forward. " Go, go!"

The ball obeyed, barely clearing the water to find the fringe and roll a few paces on the green. It proved to be a fine shot, about 12 feet below the cup leaving him with a rather lengthy birdie attempt.

Bishop also used a 9-iron and made a solid swing. The ball landed in the middle of the green, about 20 feet above the cup, leaving him a tricky speedy downhill birdie putt.

On the green Bishop stalked the putt eyeing it from behind the ball and the flag. He saw that it would be a fast one with considerable left to right break.

"Leave the pin in," he told Thornton.

Bishop's putt got on top of the swale that bisected the green and then picked up a lot of speed. It went racing down the slope and if it didn't fall into the cup it could keep going off the green thought Bishop.

Then it hit the flagstick.

A thud. And the ball dropped into the hole. Birdie two!

Bishop raised his arms triumphantly.

"You need to make your putt," he said to Cassidy gleefully as he picked the ball out of the cup.

Cassidy missed his putt as the ball slid past the cup and lost the hole.

The Hangman needed just one leg.

They halved the 17th hole leaving the match to be decided on the final hole.

– CHAPTER 21 –

TEN seconds.

Olympic sprinters can run 100 meters in less than 10 seconds.

NBA players can race up the full length of the 91-foot court to shoot a buzzer beating shot in less than 10 seconds.

Golfers are permitted 10 seconds to see if a ball will drop into the hole or not.

Tick-tock…tick-tock…tick-tock

* * *

The Hangman was still missing a leg when they came to the 18th hole, a par-4, 400-yard severe dogleg to the left called Big Bend.

Both players hit comfortable and solid tee-shots that reached the corner in the fairway, setting them up nicely for their approach shots.

On their second shots both went with 5-irons. Bishop hit a laser straight shot that hit the front of the green and rolled toward the stick. It stopped 12 feet below the cup.

Cassidy responded with his own solid and straight shot. His ball hit about pin high and kept on rolling and stopped about 20 feet above the hole.

On the green Cassidy was feeling good about his putt as he looked it over when he was momentarily distracted by seeing two men wearing bright golf shirts and hats with the Swanson Luxury Cars logo walking toward the nearby practice green.

It was Roger and Mickey, two salesmen at the dealership. They also noticed Cassidy and the two men on the green with him as they walked behind it to get in a little practice putting before playing in the charity event that was set to start in about 15 minutes.

"What is the boss doing here and not in the office," Roger said nervously.

Mickey chuckled. "The same thing the two of us are doing, getting out of work on a nice day to play golf. Don't worry."

Roger nodded, smiled and dropped a few balls on the practice green.

"Hope the boss had a nice round," he said.

Cassidy too smiled, offered a little wave to both of them and turned his attention back to his putt that if he made would likely win the hole and the game.

The putt started well but Cassidy saw it starting to drift right of the hole before stopping about a foot past. Cassidy's knees buckled a little and he dropped his putter as he watched the missed putt.

Bishop too made a smooth stroke. The ball went straight and true. Bishop began to raise his club in victory, as it rolled toward the hole. It inched closer and then it stopped literally on the lip of the cup. It rested there, defying gravity to pull it down into the hole.

Bishop stood where he was and watched. And waited.

Cassidy started softly counting. One, two, three, four…

Bishop finally started to walk to the ball, shaking his head in frustration that the ball had not dropped in.

Eight, nine, ten. Cassidy stopped counting.

Bishop stood over the ball, ready to tap it in. But, before he could touch it, the ball finally fell in.

Bishop turned to Thornton and then Cassidy and smiled. He reached down and pulled the ball out and triumphantly held it up.

"I win!"

"Wait!"

Bishop frowned.

"Strict rules of golf Mr. Bishop?" said Cassidy.

"Yeah, why?" said Bishop

"According to Rule 13.3 you have a 4 and I need to make this putt to halve the hole," said Cassidy with a sly grin.

"What the fuck are you talking about?" growled Bishop. "I have a three."

"The rule states that if the ball does not fall into the hole in 10 seconds, it is then treated as being at rest," Cassidy said slowly. "If the ball then falls into the hole before you hit it, the player has holed out with the previous stroke. Which means you have a three."

"That's right, a three. A birdie, I win the hole," Bishop said emphatically.

Cassidy shook his head slowly.

"But that player also gets one penalty stroke added to the score," he said. "You now have a 4 and I need to make this putt to halve the hole."

Bishop scratched his head and looked at Thornton who shrugged his shoulders. Cassidy calmly sank the putt.

"Four! " said Cassidy. "You can tear up that fucking Hangman of yours Mr. Bishop!"

Bishop and Thornton stormed off the green. Bishop grabbed his bag off his cart and slung it over his shoulder. He threw the bag on Thornton's cart and they sped off to screech to a stop outside the pro shop. Both got out and headed out to the parking lot.

As Bishop marched off he was muttering, " Ten seconds, ten fucking seconds."

Cassidy walked slowly to his cart looked over at Roger and Mickey who were busying themselves with practice putts at the far end of the green. Cassidy smiled, grabbed his bag from the cart and walked over to them.

"Hey guys, funny meeting you here today," said Cassidy casually.

Both picked up their heads.

"Oh, hi boss," said Mickey. "We are here for the company playing in the charity event later, you remember right boss?"

"Oh, yeah go and enjoy," said Cassidy. "It's a great day to play some golf."

"Did you have a good game, boss?" said Mickey, as the two picked up their balls and headed off.

Cassidy nodded, fiddling with his car keys.

"Yup."

– CHAPTER 22 –

STANDING in the middle of the parking lot Cassidy looked at a grim-faced Bishop. Thornton stood a few steps behind, hands on hips, a gun butt visible in his waistband.

The three of them were at Cassidy's car. Bishop had hurriedly pulled up when he saw Cassidy get to his car and now was blocking him from leaving.

"We'll take the money now. You didn't think we would leave without the $300,000, did you?" said Bishop. It was not a question.

Cassidy stared at the two. The briefcase stuffed with cash was in the trunk.

Bishop and Thornton glanced nervously around the half filled parking lot. While they had been on the course, they had been successful in not being seen by many people.

But here they and their car were out in the open as the parking lot was filling up for the charity event set to start shortly.

"Hurry," said Bishop, anxiously scanning the lot.

They had swapped their out of state license plate for a NY state one they had lifted at a truck stop before getting to the farmhouse.

But still the color and make of the car could easily be remembered and given to the police.

Cassidy opened the trunk, reached in and pulled out the briefcase. He looked at Bishop and then Thornton in the eye before handing it over.

Bishop and Thornton immediately got in their car. Bishop, in the driver's seat rolled down his window.

"There's a note at the house. Pleasure doing business with you," he said with a chuckle. "See ya around Cassidy."

Cassidy watched as they drove out of the parking lot. Then he got into his car, grasped the wheel with both hands and took a deep breath.

– CHAPTER 23 –

CASSIDY found the note under a stone at the bottom of the front door steps as Bishop promised. It was made up of cutout letters from newspapers.

She's on the 16th hole. Don't leave the house for two hours. No police!

There was also a handwritten note. Cassidy recognized Hildy's writing.

You saved my heart the very first day we met. Thank you for saving me again. I will see you soon. All my love Hildy

For the next two hours, Cassidy sat and watched the clock mumbling that the time just wasn't going fast enough.

Finally with the sun slipping down Cassidy drove back to the golf course. The clubhouse lights were on and he could hear laughter and voices as the golfers from the afternoon charity event enjoyed the traditional 19th hole festivities of drink and food.

Dressed in jeans, sneakers, thin long sleeve shirt and light jacket, Cassidy made his way on the cart path by moonlight and flashlight to reach the watery 16th hole.

Cassidy stood on the tee. It was a picturesque hole that he remembered well from the afternoon.

For the next hour, Cassidy searched every foot and corner of the hole for Hildy. He climbed up the mounds and trampled through the brush and trees surrounding each side of the pond. He looked in, behind and under the shelter that was on a rise behind the hole and was used to wait out thunderstorms. Cassidy peered into the rowboat that was moored on the shoreline with the golf mannequin dressed in bright color clothes holding a fishing rod and a line dipped in the water. He called out her name.

Nothing. No sign of Hildy anywhere. Now, Cassidy sat on the bench in the shelter in the growing darkness. He looked at his cell phone for the time and took a deep breath.

Slowly, he dialed 911.

* * *

Officer Bonner and his partner Officer Oates were the first to arrive about 30 minutes later.

"Sorry it took us so long, sir," said Bonner after introducing the two of them. "Was a bit of a walk from the parking lot and we got a little lost at one of the holes."

Cassidy nodded and quickly filled them in on Hildy's abduction and his fruitless search for her.

"No time to waste then," said Bonner. He motioned to the right side of the lake to his partner. "You take that side, I will take this side and we will meet up on the other side of the water at the green. You want to come with me sir?"

About an hour later, the three of them stood on the green. Silent. Frowns. Worried. Waiting, for more help.

Two more uniform patrolmen showed up followed by Detective Garrett and his partner Judd. Garrett took over directing the search but it quickly became evident to all that they were not going to find Hildy on or around the 16th hole.

"Are you sure, absolutely sure that this is where they said you would find your

wife?" Garrett asked Cassidy as they all stood in the middle of the green.

"Yes, yes," said Cassidy angrily. "You think I would fuck up something like where the kidnappers said I would find my wife?"

He pulled out the paper with Bishop's instructions and jammed it in Garrett's face.

Garrett put on a pair of latex gloves took it, read it, nodded, and ran his hand through his hair. He looked out at the water.

He turned to Judd.

"We are going to need some portable floodlights," he said. "And get those divers we have used before."

It was close to midnight when the divers found Hildy at the bottom of the pond near the rowboat. Under the glare of temporary spotlights they pulled Hildy's disheveled, limp body out of the water. The front of her dress was stained red. A concrete block was attached to her feet.

Sitting on the green, Cassidy could barely manage to watch, his head in his hands, shaking as they gently placed Hildy's lifeless body on the ground.

"You better call the ME, get a bus out here," Garrett said to

Judd. "And have the uniforms start putting up tape around the hole. I'll call McBain."

He looked out at the hole.

"One hell of a crime scene," he muttered. "The members are not going to like this."

– CHAPTER 24 –

THE harsh glare of the portable spotlights and a buzz of activity greeted Captain McBain as she walked up to the 16th hole. She had gotten the call at home, quickly dressed throwing on a dark windbreaker with Cable Springs Police stenciled across the back and comfortable shoes.

Yellow police tape had been put up around the entire hole. The medical examiner and ambulance staff, four uniform police officers, and Garrett and Judd stood around.

Hildy's lifeless partiality clothed body that lay under a blanket on the ground where she had been pulled out of the water.

Off in the back sitting on the shelter bench, Cassidy was not moving either staring blankly out oblivious to the commotion around him.

"Detectives what do you have?" said McBain.

"Dead white female, two gunshots, ma'am, " said Garrett. "That's the husband over there, RG Cassidy. Wife's name is Hildy Swanson. She's pretty big name around here, prominent hospital donor. Owns Swanson auto dealership."

McBain nodded, tight lipped.

"Bonner and Oates were the first ones here," added Garrett.

Bonner spoke up. "Husband called in a 911 from here. Was out looking for his wife. Babbled about some type of kidnapping."

McBain arched her eyebrows. "Kidnapping?"

She turned her attention to the body and bent down with the ME.

"What you got Doc?" she said.

"Shot twice, pretty close range," said the ME, pointing to two entry wounds on Hildy's partly bare chest, both grouped close together over the heart.

He carefully turned the body over to show two exit wounds in her back.

"Through and through," he said.

"Shot up close. That's pretty cold blooded," said McBain, "From the size of the entry wounds my guess is two guns and thus two shooters."

The ME nodded.

"Premeditated. Bastards," said McBain, standing up. "Looks like she has been dead awhile."

"She was dead weight going in. Estimated time of death," the ME said looking at his watch, "maybe 24 hours, say around 8:00-9:00 p.m. last night. I will have a better idea when I get her on the table."

McBain looked at the ground around Hildy.

"You find any shell casings?" she asked Garrett and Judd. Both shook their heads.

"Likely shot somewhere else and then dumped here last night with a 10 pound weight attached to her ankle, "said McBain, shaking her head in disgust and motioning with her hand to the concrete block attached to Hildy's leg.

Garrett looked around.

"Pretty good walk from the parking lot but she doesn't look too heavy so one of the killers could have carried her down here and the other might have had the weight," said Garrett.

McBain nodded.

"Bonner you and Oates walk back on the path to the parking lot. Maybe we will get lucky and find something snagged on a branch or on the ground, a piece of clothing from one of the killers, something," she said. "Find out if there is a manager still at the clubhouse closing up, let him know what's going on. These clubs usually have some all night security so find out who and whether they might have seen something last night."

Bonner took off with Oates. Garrett bent down.

"Dress torn," said Garrett taking a big sigh. "Any signs of rape?"

"Can't really tell until I get her on the table but my guess is unfortunately yes," said the ME. "There does seem to be some bruising evident around the face so she might have been roughed up in some sexual attack. These guys don't usually take off a woman's clothes for souvenirs. "

The ME got up.

"If everybody is good, I will have my guys take the body," he said. "I should have an autopsy report in your hands by the end of tomorrow."

Everybody nodded. The ME waved over the ambulance crew to bring the stretcher.

McBain looked over at Cassidy.

"Anybody know anything about the husband?" McBain asked to Garrett and Judd.

"Bit younger than the wife, manages the car dealership. Heard something about him being a pretty good golfer at one time," said Judd, who pulled out his iPhone and began to tap on the keyboard. A moment later he handed it to McBain.

"A most interesting guy, our Mr. Cassidy," said McBain, handing the phone to Garrett. "Let's go talk to him and find out more about this babbling."

– CHAPTER 25 –

McBAIN led the detectives over to Cassidy.

"I'm Captain McBain of the Cable Springs police department, this is Detectives Garrett and Judd, " she said to Cassidy as she sat down with the men standing. "We are sorry for your loss."

Cassidy nodded and mouthed thank you.

"I know this is tough, but we'd like to ask a few questions. First, tell us what happened from the time your wife went missing," said McBain. .

A half-hour later Cassidy leaned back.

McBain shot a look at her two detectives.

"That's some story Mr. Cassidy," said McBain. "They likely killed your wife Sunday night, they still make you play the game, you win, and they still take the money. That's pretty harsh."

"Understand at one time you were a pretty good golfer, looks like with dreams of making the pros," Garrett said. "Guess that is where the golf game comes into the story. It's definitely a new twist to the kidnapping thing. One thing it does is answer why they put her here. Pretty cruel."

Cassidy shrugged his shoulders wearily.

"Mr. Cassidy you played an entire round of golf with these two men who you said were called Bishop and Thornton. Can you describe them to us? White? Tall? Old? Young? Any scars, tattoos, facial hair?" said Garrett.

Cassidy again shrugged his shoulders and shook his head.

"I mean they looked like regular guys, " he said. "White, around my height, my age. Bishop had a brown mustache and brown hair. Think he had a tattoo on his arm. The other guy had a goatee, pretty much same color hair. They kept their hats on for the entire round."

"Did either one of them talk with an accent?" asked Garrett.

Cassidy shook his head.

"You work at a car dealership, you must see hundreds of cars, what about theirs?" said Judd. "What color, make, two doors, four doors? Any chance you saw the license plate?"

Cassidy took a big breath, closed his eyes for a moment.

"Again, nothing special about it, four doors, I think a Toyota or Subaru," said Cassidy. "Dark color. Looked pretty much like any other car out there on the roads. NY plates but didn't look at it so don't have any numbers. Sorry."

"You have had enough for one day," said McBain, standing up. "We will have a uniform to take you home. Try to get some rest. Don't touch anything more in the kitchen. We will have somebody there in the morning to secure it. We will talk more then."

Garrett waved over an officer. As Cassidy slowly walked away, McBain looked at Garrett and Judd.

"One hell of a story," she said. "Hard to make something like that up. Walk with me back to the car."

McBain headed up the cart path back to the clubhouse.

"Strange one for sure, lots of questions, the one thing we know for certain is that we got a dead woman with two bullet holes in her chest, shot in cold blood," McBain said with an edge in her voice.

"I will call the Chief and fill him in on things. I am sure he will contact the State cops and possibly the FBI as they usually need to hear about this type of crime," she continued. "We probably could use some help from both in putting out an APB on a dark car, with two men in it, just with the chance in a million that they fuck up by speeding and get pulled over. My guess is that they are not hanging around to spend that $300,000.

And the FBI can help with its database as we might as well throw in the names Bishop and Thornton with a slight chance we get a hit."

Garrett and Judd nodded.

"First thing tomorrow we get going. You two drop anything else you were working on for this. I want you to go out to the house tomorrow, check out the crime scene and talk more with the husband," said McBain.

"I will look into the financials," said Judd. "Life insurance policy, stocks, who gets what."

"Good," said McBain. "Garrett let's see if we can get a look at the husband's phone and computer logs. Start by asking him or his lawyer for permission."

McBain walked through the parking lot to her car.

"We got probably three crime scenes, here, the house and a third if as we think the wife was killed elsewhere and then dumped here," said McBain. "I will have Bonner and Oates canvas the club for staff or anybody who was playing who might have seen them on the course."

"And if she was killed somewhere else and dumped here, finding where she was held and killed is going to be like looking for a needle in a haystack," said Garrett. "There are a lot of back roads and deserted farmhouses in the area that would be a good hiding place."

McBain got into the car and rolled down the window.

"Anyway, I will have the press office release something to local TV, radio, and newspapers asking if anybody saw anything suspicious the last few days with a dark four-door foreign car and two men. Who knows maybe we will get lucky and find the needle?

And talk to the bank manager about the $300,000. That much money there should a record of the serial numbers."

She started the car.

"One hell of a story," she said.

Garrett and Judd stood in the parking lot as McBain pulled away.

"Boss doesn't look happy about this," said Judd. "She's not going to stop until she gets these guys."

Garrett nodded.

"Yeah, that's McBain."

– CHAPTER 26 –

THE sun had been down for several hours. Stars were beginning to populate the sky. Bishop had been driving since they had left the golf course with $300,000 in cash.

There was not much for Thornton to see out the window in Western Pennsylvania on this Monday night. Rolling hills, small towns, Pittsburgh ahead of them, a killing behind them. There was a modest amount of traffic, mostly trucks, heading west on I-80. Perfect for a getaway.

Thornton looked down at his iPhone and Google maps.

"Looks like there is a lake coming up on the next exit, not too far from the highway. Turn off there, we can dump this stuff," he said.

Twenty minutes later they were standing on the side of a rural road bridge over a large lake. The moon was partially hidden behind some clouds. In the growing darkness they could make out a few empty rowboats on the shore to the right, probably for fishing.

But otherwise, there was nobody around.

"Get the stuff," Bishop said.

Thornton opened the trunk. He pulled out the blanket that they had bundled Hildy's lifeless body in. There were several blotches of Hildy's blood now turned brown. Bishop yanked out the sleeping bags. He also took out a 10-pound weight.

He wrapped the blanket and sleeping bags around the weight. In a little plastic garbage bag, he put the Halloween masks and the gloves. He tied the bag to the bundle. One more look around and then he dropped it over the railing.

The pair watched it sink quickly under the dark water.

Bishop took their two guns and hurled them far into the lake.

He turned and went back to the car and came back.

"Almost forgot this one," he said, holding Cassidy's gun. He heaved it into the middle of the water.

"Glad that we got that shit out of the car," said Thornton. "Felt like death was riding in the car."

Both got back in the car. Thornton took over driving. They still had a long trip home, but it should be smooth going from now on, thought Bishop, as he looked at the briefcase that rested on the floor between his legs.

* * *

At LaGuardia Airport, Gil looked at the smattering of travelers in the Delta Lounge and eased back into the plush chair and reached for his cocktail.

He was anxious to leave New York and get home and even more anxious to get the news he had been expecting for the last few hours. His cell phone pinged.

Gil put down his drink and looked down at the text.

All went well.

He smiled. He heard his flight announced. He finished his drink, picked up his bag and briefcase, and with a little extra hop to his step walked out to his gate.

* * *

A thousand miles away in the Texas night heat, Ace rolled onto his back and closed his eyes. Next to him he heard a slight moan and an arm come across his bare chest. He looked over at the naked woman on her stomach. He picked her arm off his body.

He had lost track of time. A sliver of light snuck through the drawn curtains. It had been hours since getting back to his place, shedding clothes and inhibitions as soon as they got into the door.

They had started on the couch, rolled onto the floor and finally had made it to the bed.

He began to close his eyes again when he heard his phone beep.

Ace reached over, turned on the phone and looked at the text.

It's done.

It was the news that he had been waiting for all day.

Ace put the phone down and smiled.

– CHAPTER 27 –

BY Tuesday morning the Cable Springs police department had mobilized a dedicated force into finding the kidnappers turned killers of Hildy Swanson.

McBain had called the Chief on the way home from the golf course the night before and he had said that this was her investigation, to do what was needed, he would help out where he could and to keep him updated.

The Chief had gotten in early. He had immediately dispatched an officer and a crime scene specialist to seal off the kitchen where Hildy had been abducted texting McBain of this update. He then called the golf course General Manger with the unwelcomed news that his course was now a crime scene and would be closed for an indefinite period of time. Understandably the General Manager was very angry, complaining that it was at the start of his busy season and how could he close the course now. The Chief said sorry for the inconvenience and hung up.

The Chief contacted the state police and FBI so McBain could use them as a resource as needed but still be the lead on the investigation.

After getting home last night McBain had made one final call to wake up the Public Affairs officer to write a news releases in time for the morning news shows asking for the public's help in finding Hildy Swanson's kidnappers and killers. In particular people were asked if they had seen anything suspicious or unusual on the less traveled rural roads and isolated farms in the outer reaches of Cable Springs. Cassidy's description of a dark small car, possibly a Toyota or Subaru with two men was included in the release.

McBain had managed to grab a few hours of sleep and helped hustle the kids off to school. Before she left the house she called Garrett. Judd, Bonner and Oates to be in her office at 9 a.m.

When McBain walked into her office the four men were holding coffee cups and waiting. Judd handed her one as she sat down behind her desk.

"You are my team on this investigation, drop everything else that you might have been working on, we will be on this 24/7 from now on. We will divide up, " she told them.

The four men nodded.

"Bonner and Oates go back to the course, check with staff, pro shop and find anybody who might have seen them playing yesterday, "said McBain. "Get a list of the other golfers and start to run them down. If you need an extra set of hands for calls, let me know. Get to work."

Bonner and Oates got up and left the room.

"Detectives we went over your responsibilities last night," said McBain.

Both Garrett and Judd had already been at their desks for several hours.

Judd looked down at this notebook.

"This was her second marriage, first husband Charles died and left her with everything, so who knows that might have pissed off somebody enough to want to get back at her," said Judd.

"Money is always a good motive in a kidnapping, " said McBain nodding. "Dig a little deeper into our husband and the marriage. Was it on the rocks, any affairs, you know the score. The crime scene at the house has been sealed off. You two set up a meeting with the husband for later this morning."

"The husband said he was playing tennis at a club on Sunday when she was taken. We will run that down and see about his alibi and for Sunday night when she was likely shot," said Garrett.

McBain leaned back in her chair.

"Somebody had a reason to want her dead in a bad way," she said.

And downstairs in a dark windowless basement room, on a cold metal slab Hildy's naked body was waiting for the ME to begin the autopsy.

– CHAPTER 28 –

THE Public Affairs officer worked late into the night after getting McBain's call writing the news release asking for the public's help in finding Hildy's kidnappers and killers. She had been up before 6:00 a.m. to send it out to the morning local TV newscast and radio shows and the all-news outlets in New York City.

A few hours later, a longtime resident of Cable Springs was channel surfing while eating breakfast and heard the report on the local TV12 news station.

"Police are asking for any information in the case of the kidnapping and killing of prominent Cable Springs business woman and community benefactor Hildy Swanson over the weekend. They are looking for a dark car, possibly a Toyota or Subaru, seen on Sunday afternoon on a remote road or parked at a deserted home or farmhouse in the Cable Springs area. Two Caucasian men were in the car. Please call the following number Tip-Line (914-847-1234). All calls will be kept confidential and all tips are welcomed."

The woman frowned and a quizzical look came over her face. Didn't she see a small dark sedan with two men in it up on Wood

Lane pull into the abandoned Coarse Gold Farm when she was riding early Sunday afternoon? Hadn't that place been empty for almost a year since Old Man Sykes had died? She had heard that the kids were trying to sell it but having no luck and had let the place run-down.

She reached for her cell phone on the table. Stopped. That car could have been doing anything she thought. Maybe they were just some buyers checking out the grounds.

Do I want to get involved?

Then she thought of Hildy Swanson and the many good things she had done in the community. In fact, it was at the hospital wing donated by Hildy that her youngest daughter had been treated several years ago.

She reached for the phone and made the call.

– CHAPTER 29 –

BACK at their desks it had only taken a few taps on the computer for Garrett and Judd to pull together a summary of Cassidy's life. His parents were both deceased and he had two brothers, Randolph and Joel, living out of the area.

Cassidy had no criminal record, not even a DUI.

An internet search came up with several pages on Cassidy's golf exploits beginning as a hotshot junior and collegiate golfer. There were a few snippets of reports of a middling professional career before that apparently fizzled out. And in an Arizona newspaper there was a note of him being hired as an assistant pro at a local golf course.

Judd dug through the financials. Hildy had all the money, lots of it, left to her from her first husband Charles who had died in 2005. He had left her a significant investment portfolio, the swanky auto dealership, and homes in Cable Springs and in Palm Springs. They were waiting on the life insurance policy but Garrett was giving heavy odds to Judd that Cassidy would be the primary beneficiary.

The bank manager confirmed to Garrett the withdrawal of the $300,000 on Monday morning from the car dealership business account. Yes, the bank manager said, he had kept a record of all of the serial numbers of the bills that he could share. He cautioned the detectives, however, that since much of the money was in small bills it would be very easy for the kidnappers to use it without it being traced.

In addition to the business account, there were two other accounts the bank manager told the detectives. There was a joint checking account in Hildy and Cassidy's name with around five million and a savings account in Hildy's name of another five million. Who would get the five million in the savings account asked Garrett. The bank manager assumed it would go to Cassidy as he knew that Hildy had no living relatives.

"Take a look at this partner, " said Judd, sitting at his desk. Garrett rolled his chair over to look over Judd's shoulder at the computer screen. On it were photos and stories in all of the local and New York City newspapers of the wedding of Hildy Swanson and RG Cassidy seven years ago.

"Looks like it was news in all of the society and gossip page," said Judd. "Check out this headline, Elegance on the Hudson: Wedding of Socialite Hildy Swanson and RG Cassidy."

Judd pointed a finger at the series of photos from the ceremony and party.

"They looked like a happy couple," said Judd.

Garrett chuckled.

"Not anymore," he said.

Garrett rolled back to his desk and stood up.

"I think we have a pretty clear picture of Cassidy. Let's go pay a visit to our widower," he said. "Nice and easy."

– CHAPTER 30 –

GARRETT had calls out to the players in Cassidy's tennis practice to check on his whereabouts for Sunday afternoon. On the half hour drive over to the house, he got a call back from one of the tennis players confirming he had played with Cassidy Sunday afternoon.

As Judd turned into the driveway at Cassidy and Hildy's house he saw a security camera on a tree trunk off to the right.

"Camera," he said, pointing.

"Good," said Garrett, nodding. "In this neighborhood, where there is one camera, there are usually more."

Garrett looked out at the manicured and landscaped lawn and the stately and well maintained two level-house at the end of the circular driveway. An officer had driven Cassidy's car back from the golf course in the morning and parked it next to two other luxury cars off to the side of the driveway.

Once inside, the house was as flawless as the exterior. Cassidy had ushered them into a spacious and luxuriously appointed dining room that was dominated by an expansive dining room table that easily sat 12.

Cassidy had gotten bottles of water and put them in front of the detectives as they sat down at the dining room table. A large abstract painting covered most of the wall behind Cassidy. Behind Judd and Garrett the room opened up to a living room right out of an HGTV show featuring a full screen TV mounted over the fireplace. A large picture window occupied one living room wall with a door leading to a big patio with the swimming pool and fire pit.

If the house was immaculate, Cassidy wasn't. He looked like a mess. Two days stubble covered his face. His hair was unkempt and if he had slept it looked like he had done it in the clothes that he was wearing – a wrinkled pair of jeans and untucked golf shirt.

"Again we are so sorry for your loss," Garrett said.

"Thank you," Cassidy said softly. He looked out to the picture window and the patio and pool in the backyard.

"Another beautiful spring day," he said. "Hildy would probably be working in her garden, or maybe going for a long walk that she always liked to do about now."

Cassidy had told them that he had found the kidnappers' note and iPhone in the kitchen. Yellow police tape secured the room.

The policemen who had come in to look for fingerprints and clues in the kitchen had just left Cassidy said.

Cassidy turned his gaze back at the detectives.

"When can I get my wife back," he said quietly. "Her close friend Ali Robinson from down the street is helping with the funeral arrangements. You know that Hildy has no living relatives left.

"She wanted to be buried next to her younger sister Elsa," he continued. "She always said that. They were very close. There are pictures of both of them together all around the house. She really loved her sister."

For a second both detectives avoided looking back at him.

"The body should be released in a few days, by the end of the week for sure," Judd said. "The Medical Examiner's office will contact you."

Cassidy nodded.

There was a moment of awkward silence before Garrett started to speak only to be interrupted by Cassidy.

"You probably should know that I also have a gun," said Cassidy. Again, Garrett and Judd looked at each other. "Or should I say I had a gun."

Cassidy went through the history of getting the gun several years ago, right around the time they got the security system and then he handed the detectives his gun registration. He next told the detectives of his attempt of surprising the kidnappers on the golf course with the gun.

"That obviously didn't go too well," said Cassidy, with a shake of his head. He paused for a moment and rubbed his chin.

"You know there was a member of the grounds crew on that hole and I am sure he saw us," said Cassidy.

Garrett and Judd exchanged glances. Judd scribbled down something in his notebook.

"So you think he saw you and the kidnappers, or should I say the killers," said Garrett.

Cassidy nodded.

"What happened to the gun?" asked Judd.

"They took it from me. Guess that was a pretty stupid idea of mine," said Cassidy, who looked away and stared out the big picture window. "Guess I could have used it when they took the money in the parking lot."

"You did the right thing giving them the money," said Judd. "If you had resisted who knows you might be dead as well."

In an abrupt change of questioning, Garrett asked, "Do you have security cameras on the grounds or here in the house?"

Cassidy simply nodded.

He told them the cameras were in the backyard, outside the garage, and in the upstairs hallway outside the bedrooms.

"Unfortunately, we did not put one in the kitchen where the kidnappers took Hildy," Cassidy said in whisper.

"We still would like to look at all of the footage from Sunday," said Judd. Cassidy gave them the number of the security company.

Garrett shot Judd a quick look.

"We saw a surveillance camera as we drove up at the entrance to the driveway, Mr. Cassidy," said Garrett with just a little edge in his voice. "What about that one? Could give us a good look at the kidnappers' car at least."

Cassidy looked down at the ground and took a breath.

"Forgot about that one," said Cassidy. He took another breath.

"Unfortunately, that one is not working right now, went on the fritz just last week," he said. "Think a branch from the storm last week must have knocked it out or broke the lens. I called the company on Friday to come out and fix it. They were going to come this week."

Garrett looked at Cassidy. "I see. That's lucky for the kidnappers."

– CHAPTER 31 –

OFFICERS Bonner and Oates were at the pro shop pulling together a list of golfers and staff who were at the club on Monday and might have seen Cassidy and the killers. Bonner's phone rang and McBain was on the line telling him that they were to follow up on the phone tip of a suspicious car on Wood Lane.

"Likely a waste of time but who knows, bigger cases have turned on breaks like this, "he said leading Oates out of the pro shop and to their patrol car.

The 28-year-old Bonner was two years older and had three more years of experience on the force than Oates. They made a good partnership, sharing a similar dedication to the job and ambition of moving on to a larger city force or making detective in a few years. When they had been put on the Hildy Swanson investigation team both realized that this could be an important career opportunity.

The gravel kicked up around the squad car on Wood Lane before Oates turned in at Coarse Gold Farms on a rutted dirt driveway. Bonner noticed some tire tracks, cursing to himself halfway up the long driveway that the car was rubbing out most of the tracks making it nearly impossible for them to use the tread to try to identify the car.

As the car came up a little rise there stood a large two-story farmhouse with a wide porch that ran the entire width of the house in the front. The paint had begun to peel off the exterior and a few shutters on the second floor windows were hanging loose. To the right was a detached two-car garage with its doors open. Also to the right was a large stable and paddock area that Bonner guessed was once filled with well-groomed horses. On the left was a small riding circle for jumping with a few barriers still up. Most of the grounds were unkempt with grass and weeds knee high.

"Definitely deserted," said Oates as he pulled up to the front steps.

Bonner got out and looked around.

"Good place to stash somebody and not too far away from both the victim's house and the golf course," said Bonner as he opened the trunk.

Both put on a pair of latex gloves and unbuttoned their holsters. Bonner turned and looked at the garage.

"Door is open, let's take a look," he said.

As they got closer, they noticed the faint outline of tire tracks.

"Looks like somebody was here," said Oates as he stepped into the garage and looked around at the empty space. "Good enough place to hide a car, that's for sure."

Bonner nodded and headed back to the farmhouse. As they stepped up on the front steps, Bonner noticed several footprints in the dust. He carefully walked around the footprints to the front door that he was surprised to find unlocked and cautiously pushed open.

The interior was not much better. Dust and dirt covered the floor. There were shoe prints and the dust had been smudged in areas.

"People have been here not too long ago," said Bonner.

"Could be squatters or teenagers smoking pot or making out," said Oates.

"Or the kidnappers and killers of Hildy Swanson," said Bonner.

Standing in the foyer, straight ahead was a large staircase to the second floor.

To the right must have been the living or family room. There were a couple of chairs still in the room and Bonner could imagine a large TV hanging above the fireplace. To the left looked like the dining room with a light fixture still hanging over where the table must have been. Oates tried the light switch but as expected the power was off.

A door off the dining room led into the kitchen. There were no appliances left but there still was a kitchen table with several chairs. Bonner noticed that there was not as much dirt or dust on the table or chairs in this room.

"If somebody was here they might have sat here," said Bonner.

There was a door that went into the backyard and another one that was slightly ajar that had steps leading down to the cellar.

"You take the upstairs, I will take the basement," said Bonner.

Oates turned and went back to the foyer and then upstairs. He kept his hand on his gun. There was a large hallway with three bedrooms on the right and two bathrooms on the left. In two of the rooms an area was clear of dirt like something had been laid down on the floor.

Meanwhile, Bonner headed down to the cellar, his hand on his gun.

Standing at the bottom of the stairs he let his eyes adjust to the dim light coming through the dirty windows before turning on his flashlight. He swung the beam around. There was a chair in the middle of the room, a discarded mattress off to one side, a rust-stained sink against the far wall, and two windows on the near wall. More dust and dirt scattered around the floor and again what looked like footprints.

He walked over to the chair. Simple card table folding chair, but again he thought a little odd that it was here smack in the middle of the basement. There was no dirt or dust on it, which made him stop. Why was the rest of the room so filthy and not the chair he said to himself?

Bonner directed the light on the floor and turned it in a circle. It was just more dust and debris until he stopped the light. There in a corner on the floor was something pink. He went over and bent down. It was a piece of clothing. And there was something reddish brown on it.

Oates heard his radio crackle as he walked down the stairs.

"Dispatch, this is Officer Bonner. I need to talk to McBain. I think I found something."

– CHAPTER 32 –

GARRETT was about to ask Cassidy another question when his phone buzzed. He looked down. It was from McBain.

He answered, nodded his head a few times as he listened.

"Text me the address," he said before hanging up.

Garrett stood up.

"Mr. Cassidy we just got a possible lead on where the kidnappers held your wife," said Garrett as Judd closed his notebook and rose.

"Really?"

"Well we won't know until we check it out but if so it will definitely help. An old farmhouse up on Wood Lane, " said Garrett. "We will keep you informed."

"Good luck detectives" said Cassidy, as he showed them out the front door.

Back in the car, Judd plugged in the address and got the directions to the farmhouse. It said about a half hour from the house.

"You think it is anything?" Judd asked as he drove.

Garrett shrugged his shoulders.

"Big cases have turned on tips like this, it's at least a lead," he said.

Bonner and Oates were waiting for them outside the farmhouse when they drove up. A few moments later, McBain pulled up.

As they got out their gear, McBain couldn't shake the sense of being uneasy around Garrett or the memory of the High Country shooting. She always felt a little ache in her stomach and a clenching of her mouth around him.

But, this was no time for letting the past get in the way now McBain said to herself as she put on a pair of latex gloves. This was the biggest case since she had gotten on the force and it was sure to attract a slew of media from the city. The brutal killing of a rich socialite like Hildy Swanson was front-page material for the New York tabloids.

Headlines had never driven her at the job. It was her own inner satisfaction of knowing that she had done the job right. It was an old fashioned work ethic that she saw growing up and one that she took with her every day she put on her badge.

That the killers had so ruthlessly shot Hildy only made her more determined to bring them to justice.

Bonner pointed out the footprints on the steps and also that he had noticed more in the rooms. McBain nodded.

"Good work, Officer," she said. "Lead the way. You know where we are going."

Bonner led them to the basement stairs. As McBain stood at the bottom, she felt the hairs on her neck stand up and a bad feeling in her gut. Shining her flashlight on the chair in the middle of the room she pictured Hildy sitting, tied up, helpless and not knowing what terrible fate would await her. She noticed the mattress in the corner and shuddered at what might have transpired there.

This is where she was kept she thought. Now they just had to prove it.

Bonner pointed out the piece of clothing in the corner and McBain quickly walked over.

"Definitely looks like a piece of clothing. Wasn't the victim wearing a dress this color?" she said, kneeling as the others came up.

"Yes," said Garrett.

"We should be able to confirm that when we get back to the lab and compare this to the dress she was wearing," she said.

McBain pointed to the dark spot on the fabric.

"Looks like dried blood," she said. "If it is from one of the killers and not just the victim that will be a strong lead. Let's bag it."

Garrett handed her an evidence bag and McBain dropped the clothing in.

"Likely she was tied up here," Judd said looking at the chair. "Maybe we can find some prints."

McBain nodded, took out her cell phone and called in for the crime scene specialist to come out to the farmhouse.

Garrett went over and squatted next to the battered mattress.

"Waiting on the autopsy report on whether she was raped or assaulted. It could have happened here. We should have the crime guy check this out," said Garrett.

About an hour later while the crime scene officer continued his examination of the house, McBain and the others stood outside.

McBain turned to Bonner and Oates.

"Go see the witness," she said, giving the name and address of the woman who had called in the tip. "See if she can add any more details on either the car or possibly who was in the car. If she saw anybody in the car let's sit her down with our artist to come up with a sketch to distribute."

The two headed off to the patrol car.

"My gut says this is where they hid her and killed her," said McBain, turning to the detectives. "Put her in the car, drove over to the golf course and dumped her in the lake. Pretty neat."

"We got a few footprints from around the lake so maybe we can match them," said Judd. "That would tie the killers to here."

Tight lipped McBain nodded.

"Let's hope we get something useful off the torn dress," said McBain, who had given the evidence bag to the crime scene officer.

The three of them started to their cars.

"We still have some questions for Cassidy left," said Garrett.

"I want to sit in on this one," said McBain.

– CHAPTER 33 –

JUDD looked at his notebook as he slid into the driver's seat of the car.

"Earlier today, Bonner and Oates tracked down several of the club staff who saw Cassidy on the course and I have their notes," said Judd. "We still got time this afternoon to check them out."

"Let's go," said Garrett nodding.

At the pro shop, the detectives started with the desk staff and then had spent about 15 minutes talking with Geno of the grounds crew staff that had seen Cassidy and the others on the 16th hole. Nobody could add much to the description of Bishop and Thornton except that they looked like pretty much any other golfer.

Now they stood outside the pro shop with Jimmy.

"As the starter you saw them on the first tee, you were pretty close to them, you must have noticed or remembered something about the Bishop and Thornton fellas," said Judd pressing the point with a little frustration in his voice "Isn't there anything more that you can remember about them."

Jimmy shrugged his shoulders and took a long drag of his cigarette and blew the smoke lazily up into the air. He wore a windbreaker and hat with the Trencher's Farms logo. Jimmy was in his 60s with a weathered face from being in the sun. Told them that he had been a starter for the last five years and played 50 rounds a year.

"Guys, I see a lot of people every day. I don't really look at them closely. I just get them on the tee and off. They all pretty much look alike, same clothes, golf hat, and golf shirt. I mean one doesn't usually stand out from another. Maybe the only ones I remember are the good looking ladies," he said with a little smile.

"Ok," said Judd. "What about their demeanor? Did they talk to each other, were they friendly, not friendly."

Jimmy took his cap off and scratched his head and took another puff on his cigarette.

"I didn't hang around after I checked off their names," Jimmy said. "They were the last group going off until the shotgun start later so I headed back to the pro shop. I think I saw the Cassidy guy get into the cart with one of them and maybe they were talking a little."

Then he chuckled and added, "I figured they were talking about the bets they were going to have on the round."

Judd thanked him and told him he could leave and if they had anything more to ask they had his contact detail.

"A bit fat zero so far," said Garrett. "I don't even think it is worth it for any of them to sit down with a sketch artist. These two guys look like any of a million other golfers in the country. Shit."

Judd looked down at this notebook.

"The uniforms had found two more possible witnesses, Roger and Mickey who work at the car dealership," said Judd. "Somebody in the pro shop said that they had seen them talking to Cassidy around the practice green."

"Good, we will go," said Garrett.

The Swanson Luxury Auto dealership was a sprawling complex, with an impressive glass enclosed showroom, a massive repair shop, and a lot filled with several rows of new and used cars. It was on a stretch of auto dealerships on a major commercial street on the outskirts of Cable Springs. There was a buzz of activity when Garrett and Judd pulled in. They found Roger and Mickey at their desks in the showroom and asked them to come outside.

"We are hoping that either of you can shed some light on the two men with Cassidy or anything else that you might have seen of them yesterday," said Judd.

Roger took a deep breath.

"We were pretty surprised to see the boss at the course," he said. "He looked pretty surprised that we were there as well, though we had told him and our floor boss about a week ago that we would be out at the event."

Mickey added, "The company likes us to play in these type of community events, good to build up a little goodwill and exposure, you know."

Judd nodded.

"Mr. Cassidy came over to us after he finished, not sure he remembered that we were going to be there playing, and just told us to have a nice game," said Roger. "He said he had a good game. That's about all."

"Can you remember anything about the two men with Cassidy, their appearances, or what happened on the green," said Judd.

Roger and Mickey both paused.

"Nothing special," said Roger. "Both had hats on and we were not all that close and didn't get a good look at their faces."

"It did seem that it was a pretty intense last hole," added Mickey. "There was something going on about the last putt and the two other guys walked off pretty quickly and didn't seem to be very happy. I just figured Cassidy had won the hole and the bet."

Garrett clenched his mouth and nodded.

"Yeah, he won the round, but he wasn't a winner," he said.

* * *

Judd was finishing up at his desk at the station around dinnertime when his phone pinged. It was a text from State Police Officer Longtree asking him to meet at Sam's for a beer in a half hour. He said he had some information about the Hildy Swanson kidnapping and killing. He had left for up north on another case early in the morning and would be stopping at Sam's after his shift and they could meet there.

"You want to come," Judd said to Garrett.

"You go ahead," said Garrett. "ME finished the autopsy. I am going downstairs to the morgue to pick up the report and talk to him. You can fill me in on what Longtree had tomorrow or later if needed."

Sam's was an old fashioned bar in the middle of town near the train station. There was a lively after work crowd when Judd walked in and found a seat at the far end of the bar. He was sipping a beer when Longtree walked in, sat down and ordered a beer.

"Yeah, we were at the Trencher's Farm course yesterday afternoon, picking up a suspect on an upstate armed robbery charge," said Longtree, adding that is where he had been all day returning the suspect to the local authorities. "At the morning briefing the sergeant gave us details about the kidnapping and killing and I remembered seeing three guys coming up the 9th hole and I heard the name Cassidy mentioned."

"Anything else?" asked Judd.

"I even said something about it being such a nice day that I would rather be out there on the course with them," said Longtree with a chuckle.

Judd just nodded grimly.

"Get to the point. Could you identify them, was there anything special about them," said Judd with a sense of desperation in his voice. So far the day had yielded nothing concrete on the kidnappers.

Longtree paused and took a gulp. He shook his head.

"Hey, there were ordinary looking golfers, with hats on. Maybe one had a mustache and he could have had a tattoo on his right arm, the other I think a goatee, but other than that," he shrugged. "They were average looking, about the same size and height as the other guy."

Judd rubbed his chin.

"Let's still get you down to the station tomorrow morning first thing to sit with our sketch person," he said. "It's a bit of a reach but right now you are the best witness we have."

– CHAPTER 34 –

WEDNESDAY morning, McBain, joined by Garrett and Judd met in the Chief's office to brief him on the ongoing investigation.

Longtree had come in and was already sitting with the sketch artist in the squad room. Judd offered that it was worth the time for Longtree to come in as his law enforcement experience could provide a little more accurate description than what they had gotten so far from the other witnesses.

Garrett reported that all the witnesses corroborated seeing Cassidy and the kidnappers on the golf course on Monday afternoon. There was not much more to go on said Garrett except Geno's vague suggestion that something was a bit odd about the threesome.

"Hell yes," boomed the Chief. "The husband thought he was playing to save the life of his wife. That's not your typical 18 holes with your buddies."

The autopsy report sat on the Chief's desk. Garrett had picked it up from the ME's office last night. The report confirmed that Hildy had been killed with two bullet wounds in the upper chest area and at close range. There were no slugs in the body but from the size of the entry wounds the ME inferred they came from two different guns. The time of death was around 8:00-9:00 p.m. on Sunday night.

The report also indicated while there was no sign of rape or sexual attack, Hildy had likely put up a fight against her kidnappers. Two fingernails on both hands were broken and there were slight traces of blood and skin under several of them. The blood sample from the fingernails and bloody dress would be sent to the State Police forensic lab McBain said.

Then McBain summed up the rest of the case. The piece of clothing on the floor of the farmhouse matched Hildy's dress supporting the working assumption that she had been held and likely shot in the farmhouse cellar. A search of both the farmhouse and the 16th hole was winding down and right now there was not much to go on.

"So, what's next?" said the Chief.

"Back to the husband for more questions," said McBain getting up. "We need some answers, let's hope he can give us some."

An hour later, the three cops sat silently across the dining room table from Cassidy and his lawyer. Expecting that the police would come back for more questions, Cassidy had reached out to his and

Hildy's lawyer and asked him to come out to the house. He now sat next to Cassidy, stone faced and immaculately dressed.

Cassidy had shaved and looked like he had finally gotten some sleep. He was comfortably dressed in blue jeans and golf shirt.

McBain looked squarely into Cassidy's face and spoke quietly and firmly.

"Why don't you tell us why you couldn't have killed your wife?"

Cassidy slowly took a sip of water.

"Because I loved her. I loved Hildy more than anybody I had ever loved in the world, and possibly will ever love again," Cassidy said. "She was the best thing that ever happened in my whole stinking life."

"Everybody says they love or loved their wife," Garrett said softly.

Cassidy stared at Garrett who didn't blink. Outside it was another nice spring day.

A few chirping birds supplied a soundtrack.

"That's pretty callous Detective," said Cassidy.

Garrett nodded. "Convince us that I am wrong."

"I could never do anything to hurt Hildy. I am not sure how I can even go on living without her," said Cassidy, looking out the window. "All of this, the house, the cars, the possessions means nothing without her. That's why I couldn't have killed her."

There was a pause before McBain spoke.

"And the money?"

Cassidy looked away from McBain's stare. He took a deep breath and exhaled slowly. The lawyer who had drawn up Hildy's will also took a deep breath.

"Yes," said Cassidy softly. "All the money. I know how it must look. But all I can tell you is that I didn't kill Hildy."

Cassidy slumped back in the chair.

"We believe that your wife was killed sometime early Sunday night," said McBain. "Can you tell us your whereabouts Sunday night?"

"That night my business colleague Tyree Harris came to the house to watch a NBA game," said Cassidy.

McBain shot a look at Garrett and Judd.

"Are you telling us Mr. Cassidy that on the night that your wife is kidnapped that you calmly sat here with a colleague and watched a basketball game," she said. "That looks pretty callous."

Cassidy took another deep breath.

"I know that it looks like that, but I was afraid that if I did anything out of the ordinary that the kidnappers might suspect something. I didn't know if they were watching the house or anything," said Cassidy. "On Friday, I had invited Tyree over to watch the playoff game, have a couple of beers and hang out. We are pretty good friends and he has been over before so it was no big thing."

"What time did he come?" asked Judd.

Cassidy told them that Tyree came around 7:30, game started at 8:00 and he left a little after 10:00 when the game was over.

"I did tell Tyree that I was not going to be in the office on Monday," said Cassidy.

"Did you tell him that your wife was kidnapped?" asked Garrett.

Cassidy shook his head.

"I was worried again that the kidnappers might be watching or who knows might have placed a listening device somewhere in the house so no I didn't tell him, then," he said. "I told him on Monday right before I got to the golf club when he called. He offered to come and help but again I was too scared of what they might do if they knew I had told somebody."

Cassidy shrugged and shook his head.

"Didn't really matter, did it, " he said. "Hildy was already dead."

"Your wife was abducted while she was in the kitchen. There was no sign of forced entry on the front door," said Judd. "Did your wife usually lock the door when she was here by herself? Or could she have let the kidnappers in, known them or maybe they came as delivery people, groceries, FedEx?"

Cassidy shook his head about expecting any deliveries on Sunday, and said that since the house was set pretty far back on a quiet street, that they had gotten into the habit of leaving the front door unlocked during the day.

"Did you leave the area anytime in the last three, four months?" asked Garrett. "Alone."

Cassidy paused a moment. He then told them about his trip out west for a bachelor party about four months ago.

"What you do on the trip?" asked Garrett.

"The usual bachelor party stuff, booze and broads," said Cassidy, who gave them the names of the others and the name of a luxury resort hotel.

"Pretty ritzy," Judd said with a slight whistle, promising to contact the others and the hotel.

Cassidy nodded and told them of taking out $5,000 in cash from the bank for the trip.

"A lot of booze and broads, " he said with a grin.

They pressed him on if he could remember anything more about the two kidnappers. He had spent several hours with them on the golf course, there must be something he could remember about them in more detail, suggested Garrett.

"They were like normal guys, I mean they were just like me," said Cassidy, shrugging his shoulders. "Nothing special."

"Your wife scratched one of the kidnappers pretty good, we got blood from the farmhouse," said McBain. "Your wife was a very brave woman. One of the men must have had a cut or something on his neck or face."

Cassidy was silent for a moment. He closed his eyes.

"Yeah, one of the guys did have a cut that looked like dried blood on the side of the neck. Now that I remember it did look pretty nasty. Hildy was a tough one," he said softly, nodding his head.

"Which one?" asked McBain

"Bishop. And he had a small tattoo on his forearm. I think it was on his right arm. Looked like some type of snake," said Cassidy.

"Good," said Judd. "Every little detail can help."

McBain pulled out the sketch artist renderings of Bishop and Thornton that Longtree had provided.

"Take a look," McBain said handing them to Cassidy.

Cassidy looked them over and handed them back.

"Yeah, that's pretty much what they looked like," he said, with a shrug of his shoulders.

"Not much more here, except for the mustache and goatee," McBain said. "Pretty regular looking guys."

Cassidy nodded.

"A lot of regular looking guys in the world, " he said.

"You too are a pretty regular looking guy," said McBain with a slight smile.

– CHAPTER 35 –

McBAIN leaned back in her chair, took a deep breath and shot a glance at Garrett and Judd before speaking.

"These types of crimes usually follow a formula: a kidnap, ransom note, money exchanged and victim released without anybody seeing the kidnappers," she said. "This one doesn't."

McBain paused and again looked briefly at her detectives.

"We believe the crime was first and foremost designed as a murder and the kidnapping and ransom, which frankly was not a lot considering the wealth of your late wife, plus the golf game, was just meant to muddy the waters."

Cassidy took a long slow drink of water.

"It was almost like the kidnappers were trying to rub your nose in the entire thing. It feels like they chose you and your wife not just because you had money. This was something very personal," said McBain.

Cassidy paused and told them of his golf background, his days as a college star and then the years he spent as a pro trying to make it up to the PGA Tour.

"We found plenty of newspaper stories and more on the internet about your golf career so this would have been common knowledge to a lot of people," said Garrett.

"Anybody you played in college, or the pros that you beat, angry enough to hold this type of grudge to do something like this?" Judd asked.

Cassidy told them of not being able to sleep much Sunday night after the kidnapping and wandering downstairs to the Trophy Room.

"Hildy filled the room with newspaper stories and golf trophies," Cassidy explained sheepishly. "Looking at the photos there was a guy named Ace and a tournament at Laughlin's Fields that I remember."

Cassidy told them about the afternoon and how furious Ace was in losing and his threat to him afterwards.

"You might try him. He never really made much of it after that as far as his professional career," said Cassidy shrugging his shoulders as Judd took notes. "I guess I pretty much ended his golf dreams. I haven't seen him for probably 10 years now, not even sure where you might start to look for him. Be crazy if he did this.

But, certainly held a big grudge against me at one time. So who knows?"

McBain looked over at Garrett and Judd and then turned her stare at Cassidy.

"Can you think of anybody Hildy knew who might want to do this? Did she ever mention anybody from business, her first marriage, maybe a boyfriend before you, who would do this?" asked McBain

Cassidy took another drink of water, looked around the room again.

"Hildy several times early in our marriage talked about a stepson from her first marriage. Said he was against the marriage. Don't think he even came to their wedding. Believe his name was Gil," he said, turning to look at the lawyer as Judd took down more notes.

The lawyer nodded his head and said that indeed there was an estranged adult son from Charles's first marriage, Gil.

"I can say he was an angry man," the lawyer said slowly. "He was angry at Charles for marrying Hildy in the first place. He never trusted Hildy and thought she was only after the father's money. And when Charles died and left everything to Hildy, he got even angrier with her at the reading of the will."

"How angry," asked Garrett.

The lawyer paused.

"I think he said something like, 'I am going to get you bitch'."

The cops all looked at each other.

"Where is he now?" said Judd.

"Lives in Miami, been there last 10-15 years," the lawyer said softly. "He owned a real estate company there but had to sell half of his stake to raise money for a nasty divorce. And a lot of business projects were always a bit shaky. I heard that he always seemed to need money."

Interestingly enough he just saw Gil on Friday in his Manhattan office building the lawyer added.

"He is represented by another law firm in the building and he was downstairs in the lobby waiting for the elevator," said the lawyer. "We talked briefly. He said something about having some matters he wanted to do up here."

"So he was here in the area just two days before the kidnapping and killing?" said Garrett somewhat incredulously.

The lawyer nodded slowly.

"I have contact information for him in Miami." He gave them the details.

McBain looked long at Garrett and Judd.

"Figure that the kidnappers would divide up the money three ways, so Gil would be left with around a hundred grand," said McBain. "Not a lot in the big scheme of things when you think of the millions Hildy had. So there had to be something else."

"Revenge to finally get back at Hildy," said Garrett.

"It was a murder right from the start," Judd said.

"That would fit our scenario that the golf game was simply a ruse to throw us off," she said.

"One final thing," McBain said turning to look at Cassidy. "We would like permission to take a look at your cell phone and computer."

Cassidy turned to the lawyer.

"We can always get a warrant and be back tomorrow," McBain said firmly. "This would be a lot easier and quicker for all of us."

The lawyer bent over and whispered in Cassidy's ear.

"Fine," said Cassidy handing over his cell phone. "I got nothing to hide."

Cassidy left and came back a few minutes later with his laptop handing it over to Judd.

"I think we have talked enough today. I am sure that we will be talking more," McBain said, getting up and walking to the door followed by the detectives.

"I heard from the medical examiner this morning and I am making arrangements to get Hildy," Cassidy said quietly. "We are planning on having the funeral by the weekend."

"That will be good to have some closure," said McBain.

– CHAPTER 36 –

GARRETT stood on the front steps, running his hand through his hair, looking out at the spacious front lawn and three cars parked outside the two-car garage. McBain had already left, hurrying back to the office for another meeting.

"What you think partner?" said Garrett, turning to Judd.

Judd had been at Cable Springs for several years prior to Garrett's arrival from the High Country, having used enlisting in the Army and four years of active service in the Military Police as he way out of the Bronx. Through the Army's PaYs program that offers assistance to veterans in getting civilian police jobs he had landed the job in Cable Springs as the once lily white community had begun to grow and diversify.

Close in age, and with similar law enforcement family background, he and Garrett had quickly established a good working partnership from the start.

Judd's experience in the military made him the more analytical of the pair and a by the book cop in following procedure and building a case. He was meticulous in recording and organizing information and was always writing in his notebook.

Garrett went more by his gut and didn't mind jumping a step or stepping a little over the line when it came to tactics especially in doing interviews.

Both were driven by a shared passion of solving the crime and getting justice for the victims. They had closed a handful of homicides and robberies already but by far this was their most high profile case.

But, now adding to the pressure of being the lead detectives on the case, the partnership had begun to fray a bit around the edges the last few months. Judd felt that.

Garrett was distracted, was late many mornings, and even sloppy at times on cases and paperwork. He had called Garrett out on it a few times, hoping to clear the air but with little success.

Judd had even heard a little chatter on the streets about his partner and a gambling problem.

"So, what you think," Garrett said.

Judd took a breath, opened his notebook and looked at his notes.

"Two persons of interest. Ace, the golfer whose career was ruined when he lost to Cassidy in that tournament years back," said Judd. "Revenge, that's usually a pretty strong motive."

Garrett nodded.

"This whole golf game really throws a lot of suspicion on Ace for obvious reasons," said Garrett. "Making Cassidy play the golf game, then thinking he has saved his wife only to find out that she was already dead, well that's pretty harsh payback."

"And then we have our angry stepson Gil. He gets shut out of a big payday by Hildy when the first husband dies and then sees her with all that money fall for some down on his luck bum golfer," said Judd, with a slight chuckle. "That also sounds like revenge to me. And of all weekends, he just happens to be here."

Garrett nodded and started down the steps. He stopped at the car.

"Two people. Two suspects. Two grudges," said Judd sliding into the driver's seat. "So, we dig into Ace and Gil, right? Going to be a long night partner."

Garrett turned to Judd.

"Wrong, partner, we got one more to dig into," he said turning back and looking at the front door of the house.

* * *

Later that day, Garrett and Judd searched the internet into the lives of Ace, Gil and Cassidy.

"Look here partner," said Judd, looking at his computer screen. "Cassidy didn't say anything about his brothers, maybe this is why."

Garrett rolled his chair over and eyed the screen.

Judd had pulled up a newspaper story from The Record newspaper in Stockton, Calif. The story was from two years ago.

One Dead at Sweetwaters Robbery

Two accomplices escape and still at large

By Staff Writers

One suspect was shot and killed and his two accomplices escaped after an attempted armed robbery at Sweetwaters on late Friday night.

Patrick McCoy was shot and killed by Lathrop off duty policeman William Bounty at the adult entertainment establishment on Valley Road after the stick up. McCoy had a backpack with about $20,000 in his possession.

"Officer Bounty discharged his weapon twice, striking McCoy both times," said.

Lathrop Police Chief James Green. "Mr. McCoy died at the scene."

McCoy's accomplices fled and are still at large. Two known friends of McCoy, Randolph Cassidy and his younger brother, Joel, were questioned but were released said Chief Green.

"They told us that they were both home the entire night with a woman, who confirmed their story and that nobody left the house," said Chief Green.

The three armed men wearing ski masks entered the popular nightspot around 11:00 and quickly disarmed the bouncer and took control of the room according to witnesses.

Sweetwaters General Manager Duffy Watson was pistol whipped by McCoy and forced to open the safe. The other two men went around the room taking money from customers and performers.

McCoy was shot trying to leave the bar.

Daniel Patterson was sitting near to McCoy when he was shot.

"He went down, there was blood all over his chest," said Patterson. "One of the other men came back and stood over him. It looked like the guy who was shot was pleading for help, but the other guy just turned and walked out on his friend. It was pretty hard."

Chief Green said the investigation remained open and anybody with information was asked to contact the police.

"Well, well," said Garrett. "Looks like our Cassidy brothers are no angels."

The detectives continued to search the internet but found no more stories on the robbery or any additional runs in with the law for the brothers.

"Guess they moved from California after that," said Judd, pointing to the computer screen and several links to Denver Post stories mentioning the older brother Randolph.

It was near midnight when Garrett shut down his computer and got up.

"Time to call it a night. We will take this all to McBain in the morning," said Garrett.

– CHAPTER 37 –

THE house was still and quiet.

The clock on the wall said 2:05 a.m. Thursday morning. McBain sat at the kitchen table in a pair of her husband's boxer shorts and a New York City Marathon T-shirt from several years ago when she had qualified to run on her 40th birthday. A single light above the table broke the darkness. Her mind had been racing all night on the Hildy Swanson case so she had slid out of bed, took a quick look at the sleeping kids and came downstairs.

On the table was the case file that she had taken out of her gun safe. She usually didn't take her work home with her, wanting to shield her kids and even her husband from the often brutality of her job. But, as soon as she had stood over Hildy's lifeless and bedraggled body a raw nerve had been hit. She had seen many dead bodies through the years, but there was something about Hildy. McBain could just imagine how helpless she must have been in those final moments with two men standing just feet away ready to pull the trigger.

McBain looked at the crime scene photos and reviewed again the files with the witness interviews and autopsy report. She went over the interview with Cassidy from earlier in the day. She took a breath, exhaled slowly, rubbed her eyes and pushed her hair back off her forehead.

What would Morton do?

In her years working with Morton in the High Country, he always told her that the backbone of any investigation was to relentlessly dig for the facts. Sometimes the smallest little detail could break wide open a case he always said.

Morton also preached looking at the big picture of the case as well. The 30,000-foot look he would say. Look down at the full scope of the crime, especially the why of every case. Finding the motive most times led to discovering that piece of evidence that would unlock the entire case.

Money was historically the primary motive in kidnappings and that certainly could be the case here she thought. Hildy was rich, very rich.

On the surface this had been a successful kidnapping. The kidnappers had disappeared into thin air with $300,000. The bank manager had provided the serial numbers, but because the cash was in small bills it would be very hard for them to trace.

According to the financial records Garrett and Judd had pulled together, this, however, was just a fraction of what the kidnappers could have gotten. They could have asked for more. At $300,000 there was still plenty of money left in Hildy's estate.

Why didn't they ask for more?

Revenge was also a possible motive here. She had directed her detectives to dig into Ace and Gil and was waiting for their reports. Could there be an angry business rival or associate of Hildy involved? Plus everybody still had some doubts about Cassidy.

She put down the file, leaned back in her chair, closed her eyes and thought.

Was it money? Was it revenge? Against Hildy or even Cassidy? Was it both? Why kidnap and so heartlessly kill Hildy Swanson?

– CHAPTER 38 –

EARLY the next morning Garrett and Judd sat in McBain's office filling her in on what they had found the night before on Cassidy's two brothers Randolph and Joel including the suspected robbery in California and their living presently in Colorado.

"Interesting," said McBain after they had finished. "As you said, the Cassidy brothers are probably no angels, but at the same time it doesn't make them into killers."

McBain paused then leaned forward, putting her hands on the desk.

"Let's do a deeper dive into them. Check hotels, motels in a 20-mile radius to see if they were in the area. Go back three maybe five months. Maybe they came to scope out things. We got Cassidy's phone and computer, look at his emails, phone logs again, any long distance calls and see if he had been in contact with them," she said.

Both detectives nodded.

"What else we got going," McBain asked.

"We are going to contact the Miami police to ask them to pay a visit to our angry stepson Gil," said Garrett. "Find out a little bit more of his movements while he was here last weekend and how deep his money troubles are."

McBain nodded and mouthed good.

Next Judd said he had found on the internet two Ace Hammonds with golf backgrounds. One, however, had died in a car accident three months ago. The other worked for a club in South Texas.

"I will put in a call to the Texas Rangers to ask for their help in talking with him, see if there is anything suspicious that could tie him into this," he said.

Again, McBain nodded to the detectives and waved her hand that the meeting was over.

"Okay, let's get to it," she said.

* * *

In the midday Texas sun, the temperature was nearing triple digits. But Ace was feeling a different type of rising heat.

Today it was a black thong. Yesterday it had been red.

He smiled as Melissa bent over in her short golf skirt to place the ball delicately on the practice tee showing off a toned and well-rounded ass. Guess she forgot to wear her undershorts again he thought to himself and smiled.

He fingered his cellphone in his pocket. He had already gotten the good news he was hoping for last night. Soon he could be starting a whole new part of his life. It was looking very promising.

"Did you get a good view," Melissa said startling Ace back to the present as she stood up over the ball.

"Yes, a very good view. I could see just about everything I wanted to," he said taking off his golf hat to wipe the sweat off his forehead.

Melissa flashed a smile and slowly licked her lips with her tongue. She turned back to the ball and took a mighty swing. The ball flew straight and long.

"Should I do it again?"

"Yes, I need to take another look," said Ace with a grin.

She bent down to put another ball on the tee.

Yes, it was turning out to be a very good day he thought.

For the next half hour, the routine was repeated. Melissa would bend down to put the ball on the tee. Ace looked and smiled.

Melissa would wiggle her hips a little theatrically, swing easily and hit the ball high in the air and straight. Ace would offer a few tips on her form. When Melissa had finished the bucket of balls, they surreptitiously made arrangements to meet up later and were just leaving the practice range when two uniformed Texas Rangers walked up.

"Mr. Hammond, can we speak to you for a few minutes," said the first Ranger, a burly middle-aged man with the very appropriate name of Houston stenciled on his uniform and matching bushy handlebar mustache right out of Central Casting.

"Ma'am, would you excuse us," he said tipping his cap.

Melissa shot Ace a puzzled look, quickly collected her clubs and walked away.

The second Ranger, a long-legged blond woman, watched Melissa leave, before turning back to Ace and raising her eyebrows and smiling.

"Tough work if you can get it, I see," said Ranger Varrick.

"Just another student," Ace said weakly.

"Do you know a man named RG Cassidy?"

Ace blinked, gulped and then told the Rangers of his years playing golf against Cassidy.

"So, you and Cassidy go way back then," said Varrick. "And the last time you played him, it was not such a pleasant goodbye was it?"

Ace lowered his eyes and pawed at the ground with his spikes.

"That day he beat me at Laughlin's Fields pretty much ended my hopes of playing professionally, so yeah I remember it well and it still sucks," Ace said snapping off the words. "We were never drinking buddies to begin with and we certainly didn't hang out after that. What's this about?"

Ranger Houston told Ace about the kidnapping and killing of Cassidy's wife in New York over the weekend.

"Fuck, I was angry but not that pissed to do something like you said and kill his wife. That's crazy," said Ace.

Houston looked hard at Ace.

"Where were you Sunday night?"

* * *

It was a few hours later when Judd's cellphone rang while he was standing in the pro shop at Trencher's Farm. He had come back for one more longshot hoping that Charley McQueen, the head pro or somebody else had seen something more of Cassidy and the kidnappers on the golf course on Monday.

"Excuse me," Judd said to McQueen. "Have to take this call. Ranger Houston, thank you for calling back so soon. You talked to Ace Hammond this morning, Ranger?"

For the next few minutes Judd, nodding his head a few times, listened intently.

"And you checked out his alibi for Sunday night and this woman he said he was with," said Judd.

The Ranger said yes. Only after he had stressed to Ace the seriousness of his situation if he couldn't substantiate where he was Sunday night did he reluctantly gave them the name of the woman he was sleeping with.

"She was scared that if this became known that her marriage would be destroyed but she did confirm that she had been with Ace for several hours that night at his place," said Houston.

"Thank you again for your prompt and detailed report, Ranger," said Judd. "If you could summarize your notes and send them along that would be most helpful."

Judd gave out his office email.

"We have your contact information in case we need any follow up, thank you Ranger," said Judd clicking off his phone.

McQueen had been standing nearby through the entire conversation.

"Were you speaking about an Ace Hammond, who works at a club in South Texas," said McQueen.

Judd looked up and raised his eyebrows.

"Yes I was," he said.

McQueen took a deep breath.

"I met Ace Hammond, here at the club," he said. "He was standing right where you are detective."

Hammond had applied for the opening of assistant head pro McQueen said and after a phone interview he had invited him up to the club for an in-person second interview several months ago.

"He was here at the club for an afternoon. I took him for a tour of the course and facilities and we talked," McQueen said. "I liked him."

He told Judd that Hammond had good credentials, both from his years playing college golf and from his work at the club in Texas. He was going to call Hammond on Monday to officially offer him the job but got tied up with the charity event at the club and then the discovery of Hildy's body. Instead it was not until late Monday night when he had time to send him a quick text alerting him of his decision.

"How long was he up here?" asked Judd.

McQueen said he thought Ace was here for a couple of days looking around the area.

Judd excused himself, stepped outside and called Garrett back at the office.

"You are shitting me," said Garrett. "Son of a bitch! That's a bit of a coincidence. The Rangers never asked him if he had been up here recently?"

"I guess they never thought it was necessary once they had established that he had an alibi for the weekend," said Judd.

"Ok, let's get back on the horn with our Ranger friends pronto and ask them to go back out and talk to our Mr. Ace Hammond with a little bit more weight this time," said Garrett. "He could have come up here, scouted out the course, made arrangements for the farmhouse and hired these two guys Bishop and Thornton. Let's find out what the hell is going on here."

* * *

Rangers Houston and Varrick came back later in the afternoon and found Ace behind the counter in the pro shop. When he saw them, he was a bit surprised and then a frown came across his sun-tanned face.

"Rangers, here again, what can I do for you this time," said Ace.

"Maybe we should take this to someplace a bit more private Mr. Hammond," said Ranger Houston with just a bit of edge in his voice.

"George, can you mind the counter, "Ace said to his colleague and headed out the door followed by the Rangers.

They found a spot behind the pro shop.

"Mr. Hammond, have you ever been to a golf club called Trencher's Farm in New York?" said Ranger Varrick.

Ace had a puzzled looked. He looked first at Varrick and then at Houston but all he got back was stone-faced stares. He began talking.

Later in the day Judd took a call from Ranger Houston. He listened for a few minutes, wrote something in his notebook and then hung up. Then Judd turned to Garrett sitting across from him in the squad room.

"It's all legit," said Judd. "Hammond confirmed that he had been up here for two days, visited the golf course as the head pro said for an interview for the job. Didn't even know that Cassidy lived in the area, swore by that. I guess a happenstance."

– CHAPTER 39 –

GIL loved looking down on Miami Beach from his plush corner office high in one of the city's sleek and modern business towers.

He never got tired of gazing at the white beaches of South Beach, the blue water of Biscayne Bay and the mosaic of colorful art deco buildings and gleaming skyscrapers that gave the area a distinctive look. Gil was energized by the constant buzz of the cosmopolitan city, it's pulsating nonstop nightlife and recently the endless bounty of beautiful and exotic women.

In fact, Gil loved all the good things in life that his money could buy.

But, on a sun filled Friday morning his mood was a bit gloomier as he reviewed the projected losses of a company property. Another in a series of recent failed acquisitions left Gil with a nagging feeling in the pit of his stomach that all of this was not going to last unless his other plan succeeded.

The ringing of his cellphone roused Gil. He turned away from the window and hit answer. It was his college roommate, who he had just seen on Sunday in New York.

"Gil, real quick, got some news for you," he said.

"Guess it has got to be big news for you to be calling after just seeing you a few days ago, " said Gil.

"Your ex-stepmother Hildy is dead," he said. "Killed in a kidnapping according to the TV and papers. They found her Monday night. Pretty gruesome stuff, shot a few times."

Gil closed his eyes, paused and let a little smile cross his face.

"That's awful, "said Gil. "Shot and killed in a kidnapping, who would want to do such a thing to her?"

"Didn't you have a real blow up with her years ago?" said his friend. "What did you used to call her, the bimbo who fucked you out of all of your money?"

"That was years ago. Haven't thought of her in years," Gil said. "Thanks for the heads up. Got to go, talk soon."

Gil spun around in his chair, stuck his feet up on the window and looked out at the idyllic scene below.

A rush of memories flooded his mind.

He was a little boy, laughing and holding hands with his mother. They were at Disney World, skipping through Fantasyland, squealing with delight as they rode all the rides.

He remembered thinking of his mother as a queen. She was always so elegantly dressed and would dress him up as well to take him to Broadway shows and the opera.

Gil was a young teen when the joy turned to sadness. He stood shivering in the January cold, gripping his father's hand as his mother was buried after losing her fight to cancer.

The next few years were all about father and son time and were happy ones for Gil in high school. The bond between them grew so strong that Charles took him on many business trips so Gil would not be at home without a parent.

Then Hildy came along. Pretty, effervescent and very young. Charles was enthralled with her. Gil only saw her as a gold digger, mesmerizing an older man with her attention and body. As their relationship grew, Gil's anger with his father and resentment of Hildy boiled over. He pleaded and fought with Charles not to get involved with Hildy, that she was out to get his money. Even on their wedding day, Gil was in Cancun with his buddies drinking and screwing the entire weekend. Gil moved to Miami and never saw Charles and Hildy while they were married.

After his father died, he remembered vividly the pristine conference room and him sitting at the table with the lawyer and

Hildy for the reading of Charles' will. When he heard the news that all of Charles' estate would go to Hildy and nothing for him, Gil exploded, spewing curses and threats at Hildy as he stormed out of the room.

The phone on his desk jarred Gil back to the present. He turned and pushed the speaker button.

"The Miami police are here, security just called from the lobby, they want to see you, Mr. Swanson, " said his secretary Iris.

Gil paused and took a deep breath.

"Send them up," said Gil

A few minutes later his secretary opened the office door.

"The Miami police are here, Mr. Swanson," said his secretary.

"Iris, show them in," said Gil. "I know what this is about."

In stepped a middle-aged man and younger woman.

"I'm Detective Coburn and my partner is Detective Rodriquez," said the man as the pair took seats across from Gil. "The police up in Cable Springs, New York have asked us to talk to you about your relationship with your ex-stepmother Hildy Swanson, who was murdered a few days ago."

For the next 30 minutes, Gil told them about his fractured relationship with his father over his marriage to Hildy and his worries that she was just after his money. He admitted that he had been angry with Hildy when he had been shut out of his father's Will.

"How angry?" asked Coburn.

Gil smiled.

"Angry, but not angry enough to kill her," he said.

"We understand you were up in New York last weekend. Where were you on Sunday night?" asked Rodriquez.

Gil smiled.

"Sunday night, had room service and was in my hotel room at the Hilton," said Gil. "All night."

"Anybody with you," said Rodriquez.

"No, unfortunately I was alone," said Gil.

Both detectives raised their eyebrows and exchanged quick glances.

"That's too bad Mr. Swanson, as your ex-stepmother was killed on Sunday night," said Coburn.

* * *

A few hours later in the squad room Judd opened his notebook and briefed Garrett on what the Miami cops reported from their interview with Gil.

"He came clean that he didn't like Hildy but again not to the point where he would go to kidnapping and murder," said Judd.

"Revenge in getting back at Hildy by killing her and getting her money sounds like a strong motive to me," said Garrett. "And the lawyer said that Gil needed money."

"From outside appearances money does not seem to be a problem," Judd said of the Miami cops report of the company offices occupying a full floor in a prestigious high rise. "But again that is not what the lawyer said."

Garrett took a deep breath and ran his hand across his mouth.

"Try this one out partner, " he said slowly. "Gil needs cash. Cassidy wants more cash. The two of them in this together."

Judd nodded.

"Each has a reason for wanting Hildy dead," he said with a slight chuckle.

"What he say about him being here last week," said Garrett.

"According to him, he had to come back to make some changes to his Will with his lawyer after the divorce and to see some old friends on Sunday afternoon," said Judd.

"And Sunday night," said Garrett.

"Was in his hotel room in the city all night at the midtown Hilton," said Judd. "Alone."

Judd closed his notebook.

"You put everything in that damn notebook of yours, don't you," said Garrett.

Judd nodded.

"It might just be a coincidence, Gil being here on the weekend, " said Judd.

Garrett looked hard at Judd.

"The angry estranged son is around just a few days ago when the wicked stepmother is kidnapped and then shot in cold blood," said Garrett, shaking his head. "I don't believe in coincidences, not when it comes to murder. We keep digging."

His cellphone pinged. He looked at the text.

"26 days" - Rudy"

– CHAPTER 40 –

ON Friday afternoon the Chief called in McBain and her two detectives for a briefing on where the Swanson investigation stood. It had been four days since Hildy's body had been dragged up from the water.

"What's the husband been up to, anything suspicious," said the Chief.

"We have had him on 24 hour surveillance. Bonner and Oates sitting on him," said McBain. "Nothing out of the ordinary. Went to the funeral home to make arrangements, the funeral is Saturday. Had a few people come to the house for we figure condolence calls?"

There was silence in the room before McBain continued.

"Other than that, Cassidy strikes me as a smart guy, sure that he knows we are keeping an eye on him so don't think he will do anything stupid, but we will continue to sit on him in hopes he might do something careless."

Garrett filled the Chief in on Cassidy's two brothers and their possible involvement in an armed robbery in California. And if the two had been in the Cable Springs area recently, a canvassing of local motels and hotels had come up empty. Cassidy's phone logs and emails showed no evidence that he had been in touch with his brothers.

Again, the room was quiet.

"What about the two other suspects? Thought you said you had some good leads on tying them into this thing," said the Chief.

Judd told the Chief about the Texas Rangers interview with Ace and that his alibi for Sunday night was corroborated and his story about his trip to Trencher's Farms several weeks ago was pretty solid.

"He's still plenty angry at Cassidy but right now we don't think he is involved," said Judd.

"And the other one," said the Chief.

"We had the Miami police interview Gil yesterday at his office. We are still doing a little digging," said McBain. "He's got some money problems at his company and a bad divorce that gives him motive plus he holds a grudge against Hildy for getting all of the father's money. He doesn't have a strong alibi for Sunday night."

The Chief raised an eyebrow.

"He's here in the area and nobody can vouch for where he was the night Hildy gets shot?" said the Chief.

"He told the Miami cops he was at the Hilton in Manhattan in his room all night, alone, and called in room service," said Garret. "We are checking into the room service at the hotel to see if we can nail that down. Plus, we are going to make some calls to some people he has done business with. See just how big of a money problem he has."

"Any forensics?" said the Chief.

"Waiting on the blood report from the dress in the farmhouse," said McBain. "Other than that, nothing. Farmhouse was clean. Remarkably clean. They were very, very careful. If that is where they killed her, they picked up the bullets and shell casings. We have an idea the type of guns but besides that nothing. And more than likely those guns are sitting at the bottom of some lake who knows where."

The Chief clenched his mouth and slowly nodded.

"How about where they dropped the body?"

McBain shook her head again.

"Golf course, Christ, there was millions of fingerprints on every cart and we couldn't use any of them. Couple of footprints. Two average size guys from what we could determine. There are only a few million of those walking around so that's not really going to help. Right now we've got nothing!"

"Anything on the street from your snitches on who these bastards might be," said the Chief looking at his detectives.

Judd shook his head.

"Quiet on the street," he said. "These two blew in and out like the wind and could be blowing anywhere right now. With a lot of dough in their pockets."

"Shit," said the Chief, slamming his hand on his desk. "Everybody has a big fucking nothing. Dead ends all."

The Chief leaned back in his chair and took a deep breath.

"Ok, let's follow up with the estranged son and his business dealings, see where that leads us. We will wait for the blood report to come back. Continue to sit on Cassidy.

Maybe we will get lucky and get a break," said the Chief.

* * *

In the upstairs bedroom a naked woman was sleeping on her stomach. A sheet covered her up to her waist. She had long brown hair past her shoulders. Her clothes were scattered around the room. Two used discarded condoms were also on the floor next to the bed.

Under the mattress was $300,000 in small bills in neatly stacked bundles.

Downstairs Bishop and Thornton were sitting on the couch in the living room. The only light came through the open door from the kitchen. The clock above the stove said 2:30 Saturday morning. Bishop had a Rockies tee shirt on. Thornton had thrown on a pair of boxers. Half-empty beer bottles were on the table and a few roaches were in the ashtray.

"You think everything is ok," said Thornton.

"Everything is cool," said Bishop taking a gulp of beer. "We left the cops no trace. They have no fucking clue and have no fucking way of finding us. We are good."

Thornton nodded.

"Ok, still get a little worried man," he said. "This is our biggest score and we don't want to fuck it up. You are right, there is no way the cops can find us. The guns are in some lake in Pennsylvania. Nobody can really ID us from the course."

Bishop smiled, reached for his beer bottle and stood up.

"Now I think it is time we move on back upstairs," he said. "That is an expensive fuck up there waiting for us."

– CHAPTER 41 –

THE Saturday morning sky was a flawless blue, a stark contrast to the throng of mourners in black who stood two and three deep around the family plot of Hildy's parents and her sister Elsa. Hildy's mahogany coffin was placed next to her sister's grave. The Oak Grove cemetery was the biggest in Cable Springs and it was immaculately manicured with the towering oak trees scattered around the grounds giving ample shade to visitors from the brilliant sun. The limousines were a polished black.

Friends from all parts of Hildy's life had turned out for the funeral. There were college friends from Skidmore, others from the upper reaches of Manhattan society, and even a few had flown in from her winter home in Palm Springs. Work associates, including Tyree and others from the car dealership, stood silently around the grave next to members of the hospital board and Dr. Steiner. Clergy and civic leaders mingled in the crowd.

Neatly dressed in a dark suit, white shirt, dark tie, and dark sunglasses, Cassidy talked and greeted most, getting hugs from the women and warm handshakes and a pat on the back from the men. In addition to condolences many of them softly urged Cassidy to leave the nightmare of Hildy's death behind and move away from Cable Springs as quickly as possible.

"It's not going to do you any good to stay around here with all of the memories of Hildy everywhere," said Tyree, putting his hands on Cassidy's shoulders. "Get out of here and find a place quiet and far away to take some time to clear your head of this tragedy. Don't worry about the business we will keep it in good shape."

Cassidy brushed a tear or two from his eyes and his voice choked up a little. "Thank you, my friend, that sounds good," he said. "Just get in my car and go and leave this sadness behind for awhile. I still have some golfing buddies from my old course in Arizona, maybe go there and sit in the sun and not think about this."

Tyree nodded. "Do it, it will help you heal."

The service began with the minister from the main church in town leading the mourners in prayer and reminding them all of Hildy's generosity in giving back to her community. The Cable Springs Mayor stood up next and she eulogized Hildy for her outstanding contributions to the town.

Watching off to a side under a large oak tree stood Garrett and Judd.

Garrett's phone pinged. He looked down.

"25 days-Rudy"

Garrett quickly deleted the message and looked out at the funeral.

Since the ultimatum from Rudy on Monday, Garrett had been searching for ways to come up with the $15,000 by the 30-day deadline. So far he had come up with a big fat zero.

Could his funeral be next he thought to himself? Garrett knew that ending up dead was not such a far-fetched possibility in his situation. It had been only a few months ago that Garrett had seen the most recent suspected handiwork of Rudy.

The dead man had been shot twice in the back of the head, up close and execution style. In a message to the community that you either pay up your debts or suffer the consequence, the Asian-American man had been dumped into a large garbage container behind a popular Chinese restaurant in town.

One thing was for certain his funeral wouldn't be this big Garrett said to himself with a chuckle.

"Hey, partner maybe the Doc has some ideas of who might have wanted to do this," Judd said of Dr. Steiner who stood up next and recalled the story of Hildy's passion and persistence in bringing to life the special wing in the hospital in her sister's name more than 20 years ago. When he finished he placed a bouquet of flowers on her casket.

Garrett pushed Rudy out of his mind and nodded.

"Yeah, worth a chat," he said.

At the end of the service, Cassidy placed a handful of flowers on the top of the casket.

Hildy was lowered into the ground next to her sister.

The mourners watched silently before turning to head back to their cars. Garrett and Judd went up to Dr. Steiner.

"Sir, I'm Detective Garrett, this is my partner Detective Judd of the Cable Springs Police department. We are investigating the death of Hildy Swanson. Could we have a moment?" said Garrett.

"Of course," said Dr. Steiner.

"How well did you know the deceased?" asked Judd.

For the next few minutes, Dr. Steiner told the detectives about meeting Hildy, her funding for the creation of Elsa's Pavilion for

Infectious Diseases at the hospital in memory of her sister and continued involvement ever since.

"She is our most important benefactor and without her none of this would be possible. We have saved countless lives and will continue to do so with our research in this field because of Hildy." said Dr. Steiner. "She was truly a wonderful person."

Garrett and Judd both nodded.

"Do you know of anybody would want to harm her?" asked Garrett.

Dr. Steiner took a deep breath and looked back at the gravesite where the grounds staff was filling in the grave with dirt.

"Everybody liked Hildy, what was not to like about her, she was warm, generous to a fault," said Dr. Steiner. He paused and frowned. "I did hear Hildy once talk about a stepson from Charles' first marriage who held a grudge against her, over the family money when Charles died."

Garrett shot Judd a look.

"Do you remember a name?" asked Garrett.

Dr. Steiner ran his hand across his mouth.

"Yes, I think so, Gil," said Dr. Steiner. "Yes, it's Gil."

Garrett and Judd both nodded.

"We are aware of Gil and his animosity over the years to Hildy over being left out of his father's will. Did you ever have any dealings with him or see or hear him say anything threatening to Hildy," said Garrett.

"I never met Gil, but I do recall that shortly after Charles' death Hildy came to assure me that there would still be sufficient funding for the hospital wing. At that time she told me she had been upset and frightened by the stepson's anger at her when the Will was read, " said Dr. Steiner. "She said something like she was glad that he lived in Miami and hopefully would stay away from her."

"Thank you Doctor, you have been very helpful," said Garrett.

Dr. Steiner nodded. As he walked away, Garrett heard him say something about a promise kept.

– CHAPTER 42 –

TWENTY-FOUR hours after Hildy's funeral, Judd was in the squad room working the phones.

Judd never liked Sundays when he was working a case.

It was hard to talk with people. Most of the time they ignored their phones instead spending time on recreational activities with friends and family. On this Sunday morning, those who Judd managed to get hold of were either reluctant to speak about Gil's financial problems or didn't have much more to add except that some of his business ventures had not panned out.

Except for Sandy Watson. Watson had worked with Gil for almost six years before leaving the Miami real estate firm and moving to New York more than a year ago. Watson was more than happy to share more details on Gil's money woes.

"Gil has a mess of trouble right now," said Watson, who had just finished an early round at his golf club on Long Island. "I saw the writing on the wall. When I left, Gil had already made some bad investments on a few big projects in Florida and what I have heard things have gone from bad to worse recently."

Judd was busy taking notes at his desk in the nearly deserted squad room. Garrett had gone into the City to verify Gil's alibi of being in his hotel room all last Sunday night.

"You said it's getting worse," said Judd.

"About six months ago, he finalized a bad divorce. The ex busted his balls for every dime she could," said Watson. "He was hemorrhaging money then. Now on top of that shit, he's got a business loan that he has got to start making payments on shortly that is going to cost him a ton. Word on the street is that he might even have trouble making the first payment."

Judd kept on taking notes in his notebook.

"How much does he need?" asked Judd.

Watson paused, took a big breath.

"I'm not exactly sure, I think it is around a half million," he said slowly.

"And if he doesn't come up with the money?"

"Maybe Chapter 11. It could get real ugly, real quickly, " said Watson.

Judd put down his pen.

* * *

It was nearly 4:00 later that afternoon when Garrett sat across from Judd in the squad room to fill his partner in on his investigation of Gil's alibi of spending last Sunday in his midtown Hilton hotel room.

Garrett had spoken with the room service staff member who said Gil had come to the door to get his dinner around 9:30 that night. Room service also confirmed that the dinner tray had been picked up outside his room at 11:30 p.m.

Judd looked at the autopsy report.

"So, Gil was in his room around 9:30 that night. The medical examiner thinks that Hildy was killed around 8:00 p.m." he said.

"It took me about an hour to drive in and out on a Sunday morning," said Garrett. "Figure around the same on a Sunday night. He could have left the farmhouse at eight or bit earlier, and still be back at the hotel to order room service at nine. It's doable."

The massive block long hotel has more than a dozen entrances and exits added Garret.

"He could have easily gone out one of them without being noticed," said Garrett.

"How about security footage?" asked Judd.

Garrett shrugged his shoulders.

"I checked out several hours of footage and didn't see him. But, he could have

just pulled a hat down on his face or shielded his face so we couldn't identify him," he said.

Gil had not parked a car in the garage said Garrett and there was no record of him renting one from any of the major agencies.

"If he left and came up here he could have taken a taxi, an Uber, gypsy car, who knows," he said. "It would be a bit of a risk if he did that as the driver could easily ID him, but maybe he just pays him off to keep quiet."

Judd nodded.

"Remember, after he has brunch with his friends, which ends around three, Gil says he walked around the city a little bit, and then comes back to the room, but he has nobody who can confirm his whereabouts for those six hours," said Judd. "He could have left then, come up to the farmhouse, met with Bishop and Thornton to make sure everything was going according to plan and then come back."

Garrett nodded.

"It's doable."

– CHAPTER 43 –

GARRETT trudged into the station house a little after 7:00 Monday morning. He had a styrofoam coffee cup in one hand and a donut in the other. He acknowledged the night shift officer behind the front desk with a slight nod. The squad room was largely deserted with only a skeleton night crew still working and the day shift starting in another hour.

After leaving Judd the night before, Garrett had a restless and troubled night at home alone with his drinking and thoughts. He had racked his brain trying to figure out an answer to coming up with the $15,000 he owed his bookie. The idea of driving to Canada or even flying out of the country had entered his mind. But he still didn't have a real plan as he sat down, clicked on his computer, and sipped his coffee.

About 15 minutes later, the email notification box appeared in the upper right corner of Garrett's computer.

NYSP Crime Laboratory System

Garrett clicked it open. It was addressed to McBain and Judd as well. It was the report on the blood sample taken off the dress in the farmhouse.

The lab report was pretty standard verifying that it was human blood type B negative. Since Hildy's blood was O positive it only confirmed their premise that she had fought off one of the kidnappers and badly scratched him.

One tough broad Garrett said to himself as he took a deep sigh, hit the print button, and got up and walked across the room to the printer. He would put this into the casebook along with all of the other reports and notes they had gathered so far.

Back at his desk, he scanned the report again. There was a footnote at the bottom stating that B negative was a very rare blood type and found in only approximately 2 percent of the population. Garrett looked at that and sat down. A quizzical look came across his face. In the back of his mind there was something about B negative blood that he remembered seeing recently.

Garrett leaned back in his chair and closed his eyes. Think dammit he thought. What did you see?

And then it hit him. He opened his eyes wide.

Garrett began to rifle through the casebook until he came to what he was looking for. He smiled and slowly read it, once and then a second time.

It was a story they had found on a LexisNexis search of newspapers and websites as part of a wide background investigation of people of interest in the case.

Garrett looked at the lab report again and smiled.

That son of a bitch he thought. Now it began to make sense on how they did it. Ingenious, but not smart enough he said to himself. One stupid mistake and the entire plan cracked wide open.

Garrett took out his notebook and wrote down a name and a hometown.

There was another beep on his phone. Garrett looked at the text. "23 Days- Rudy."

He quickly deleted the text. A thought came into his mind. He leaned forward and looked at the lab report and at the casebook again. A slight smile crossed his face. He looked around the nearly empty squad room.

Garrett took the copy of the newspaper story out of the three-ring binder, folded it, and put it in his pocket. He pulled out a pack of matches he had in his office drawer and then casually walked through the squad room and outside. There was a little smoking area to the left of the station's front door with one of those big cigarette butt garbage containers.

Garrett looked around and didn't see anybody in the parking lot or coming out of the door. He put a match to the paper, let it catch, and then dumped it into the container.

He smiled.

* * *

Cassidy too had been up early. His bedroom was strewn with clothes.

When he got downstairs, he made a cup of coffee, wolfed down a quick breakfast, and settled down at the kitchen table. The yellow police tape had been taken down leaving no sign of the kidnapping that had taken place in the room.

The first call he made was to the lawyer. They talked for about a half hour and arranged to meet at the house the next morning to complete all the paperwork.

Cassidy took a sip of coffee and crossed off the lawyer on his list of calls to make. He looked at who was next and started to dial. It took nearly two hours for him to get to final name – Tyree.

The friends talked for a few minutes before Cassidy suggested Tyree come over the next night for drinks.

"Nothing special, just thought it would be nice for us to get together again,"

Cassidy said in closing.

* * *

Judd saw the lab report email when he came in the midafternoon. He made a quick comment to Garrett that it confirmed their suspicions that Hildy had attacked one of her killers before being shot in the farmhouse. But, besides that it didn't help in identifying the killers said Judd. Garrett nodded.

For the rest of the day, Garrett and Judd busied themselves with a home invasion from the previous night. First, they went out to the house to interview the frightened husband and wife and show them some mug shots. They spent the rest of the day hitting the streets to see if they could dig up any information on the perpetrators.

That night Garrett sat in the dark at home drinking and thinking. But this time he had a plan.

– CHAPTER 44 –

TUESDAY morning, Cassidy left the bank and walked to his car through a light drizzle carrying a black gym bag. He had gotten to the bank shortly after it opened and spent about an hour going through several safety deposit boxes.

He knew it was going to be a busy day so he hurried home for his appointment with his lawyer. Before the lawyer arrived, he carefully put away the black gym bag in the master bedroom.

The meeting took about an hour at the dining room table, Cassidy signing all of the necessary papers as a paralegal from the lawyer's office witnessed.

"Thank you for all of your help these last few days and for all of the many years you managed Hildy's matters," Cassidy said, shaking the lawyer's hands as they stood on the front steps. "I know you'll take care of Tyree at the dealership. He's a good man, certainly ready for the job. And I feel comfortable leaving things in your hands while I'm gone."

The lawyer nodded.

"Thank you. Working with you and Hildy for these many years has been a pleasure and a privilege," said the lawyer. "When the insurance funds and estate funds are available I know where to deposit them and will contact you immediately. Don't worry about things while you are gone. I will be here when you get back."

Cassidy looked out at the cars parked in the driveway and took a deep breath.

"Yes, when I am back," he said quietly as the lawyer got into the car and left.

An hour later, Cassidy walked into the police station, casually dressed and relaxed.

He sat down across from Garrett. Judd was in court testifying on a previous case. Cassidy took a deep breath and spoke slowly.

"I have been thinking a lot wandering around the big empty house. At the funeral, people were telling me that it would be good for me to get out of town, leave the horror of Hildy's death behind," he said. "I think it's a good idea. I don't think I can handle staying here much longer."

Garrett nodded. "Don't blame you, not a lot of good things to remember about this place anymore."

"This morning I gave the power of attorney to the lawyer to take care of everything, "said Cassidy. "I talked with a real estate agent about the house and probably going to put it up for sale at some time, but will make up my mind later. The lawyer is working on putting a plan in place for the car dealership. He will figure it out."

"When you leaving?" asked Garrett.

"Tomorrow, before lunchtime I figure. No reason to wait around. Just throw some shit in the car and go."

"Any place in particular?"

Cassidy shrugged his shoulders.

"Just point the car in a direction and drive. South, North, West, who knows? Who gives a shit, anyplace but here," said Cassidy.

Garrett nodded as Cassidy stood up and reached out to shake the detective's hand.

"Thanks for all of your hard work and efforts. Maybe someday we will find these bastards. My lawyer will know how to reach me if you get any news."

Cassidy turned and started away.

"You seeing your brothers?" asked Garrett.

Cassidy stopped. He looked down for a second, took a deep breath and turned around to look at Garrett, who was staring intently at him.

"Wasn't planning on it," he said. "Haven't seen them for several years now. Why you ask?"

"In times of stress and pain, lots of people want to go back to family for comfort and support, that's all," said Garrett.

Cassidy nodded.

Garrett watched as Cassidy walked out of the station. He smiled.

Garrett's phone beeped. He looked down. It was a message from Rudy. "22 days."

Two hours later, Garrett walked into the Chief's office, shut the door and sat down. He got up after twenty minutes.

"You will tell Judd and McBain, " Garrett said standing at the door of the office. The Chief nodded.

It was early evening when Garrett left Walmart with a small package that he had gotten in the electronics section.

In his car, he pulled out his phone.

"I want to talk. Tonight at eight o'clock at the Irish House off Route 22," he said.

* * *

Garrett was working on a Corona at the bar when Rudy sat down and ordered a Budweiser.

"Looks like Jimmy's down in Katonah," said Rudy looking around the dimly lit bar with a pinball machine tucked in a corner and a juke box in the other. There were just a few others in the bar.

"I am taking some time off, leaving the area, tomorrow," said Garrett.

Rudy took a quick gulp of his beer, put the bottle on the bar and bent in closer to Garrett.

"You're not trying to pull any shit on us are you Garrett," he said in a sinister whisper. "If you are trying to run on us, I will track down your sorry ass and hurt you, that's a promise."

Garrett smiled.

"Relax Rudy," he said, patting Rudy's shoulder. "Why would I tell you I am leaving if I was trying to run out on you? Right? Wanted to let you know so you wouldn't go ballistic if you didn't see me around for awhile and come hunting for my ass."

Garrett took a slow drink.

Garrett told him the story, his theory and his plan.

Rudy raised his beer and took a long drink. He nodded.

"It just might work Garrett and save your no-good ass," he said.

"Good," said Garrett, smiling. "I will let you know when I am heading back."

Rudy turned to Garrett and chuckled.

"Wait, you think I am going to just let you go, no fucking way," he said.

Rudy took another gulp. "Plus you know, I could use a little time away from my wife who is busting my balls about her father and finding a rehab place for him. Let her figure it out, it's her fucking father. Who knows maybe I can come out ahead in this as well? Nope, Garrett, I am coming with you."

"Your call, "Garrett said quietly. "I will pick you up at nine at the usual spot tomorrow."

Watching Rudy lumber out Garrett thought to himself it might be good to have a big guy with a gun along where he was going.

* * *

It was past midnight when Garrett rolled to a stop on a tree-lined street in an upscale neighborhood of town. He clicked off the lights and turned off the car. The street was quiet, middle of the night, so no surprise. Nearest streetlight was several houses down.

He pulled out a small box and his flashlight. Closed the door gently and began walking.

He stopped at the end of the driveway. No lights on in the house. No lights on in the houses across the street or next door. He started up the long driveway. There were two cars parked outside the house. He took out his pen flashlight and peered into the first, a snazzy sports car.

Garrett bent down and crawled under the rear bumper. The Spacehawk tracker was small, about six inches and magnetic. He attached it to the underside of the car and was done in less than 10 minutes.

He turned off his flashlight, walked back to his car and checked his Google maps app on his phone and smiled.

– CHAPTER 45 –

CASSIDY stood on the front steps and soaked in the May sunshine and warm temperatures early Wednesday morning and thought what a perfect day for a drive. His Navarra Blue Audi A5 coupe was parked in the driveway. He had packed up the car last night, anxious to get going as soon as possible. It would be good to get away he thought as he slid into the driver's seat.

As he pulled down the long driveway, he took a long last look in his rearview mirror at the house. There had been some good times there he admitted.

Driving down the street, Cassidy didn't notice a grey RAV4 pull out from the curb down the block. Two men were in the car.

* * *

It took Cassidy about 90 minutes to get over the Hudson River and start west on I-80, the second longest Interstate in the country at 2,900 miles across America's midsection. Cutting through 11 states from Teaneck, New Jersey to the Golden Gate Bridge in San Francisco, the highway raced through the Great Plains, up the Rockies before making a run to the Pacific. This concrete ribbon passed through or near Chicago, Omaha, Des Moines, and Cheyenne.

But, Cassidy had only eyes for the white line on the roadway. The roadside motels, truck stops, and occasional billboards were pretty much a blur to him.

As the miles sped under his wheels, Cassidy's mind raced back through his life.

There were the highs in the early years on the golf course when the local papers ran headlines following his rise up through the junior ranks and then into college. But the newspapers stopped writing about him as his career stalled out after college.

The following few years were the low point of his life. Cassidy fell into a dark place filled with frustration, disappointment and drinking. It had started when his first love Carol turned down his marriage proposal. The idea of spending the rest of her life with an assistant golf pro was not very appealing she coldly told him that last night. She had bigger ambitions and goals Carol said starting with pursuing her life's dream of being a fashion model. A prestigious agency in Paris had offered her a job she said walking out of the apartment and his life.

But, the kindness and tenderness of Hildy and her unwavering love for him pulled Cassidy back from the abyss.

He cranked up the music. It was the Allman Brothers, "Ain't Wastin Time No More."

Ain't that the truth he said tapping to the music on the steering wheel and singing along.

He put his foot down harder on the gas. Several miles behind, the driver in the grey RAV4 put his foot down harder as well.

– CHAPTER 46 –

CASSIDY did about 9 hours and close to 600 miles a day.

He stopped the first night outside of Toledo. It was a Motel 6. He paid cash. A half hour after checking in he grabbed a burger and couple of beers in a nearby diner. Back in room 22 on the second floor, Cassidy quickly fell asleep, his clothes and black gym back thrown on the other bed.

On the floor above, the two men in room 30 had watched a Reds game on TV and brought in some fast food. One man won $25 in a bet. As he pocketed his winnings from his traveling companion, he thought first bet I have won in a while. The men took turns sleeping for two hours while the other stayed awake. A cellphone that stayed on all night was placed on the night table between the two beds.

The following night Thursday, Cassidy made it to Des Moines and paid in cash for room 35 at a Hampton Inn just on the outskirts. He sat at the lounge bar, mindlessly watched something on ESPN while watching the waitress' legs. Like the night before clothes and a black gym were tossed on the other bed.

The grey RAV4 was parked down the street at the American Inn. The two men were in room 12. The big burly guy paid for the

In-Room movies and watched a porn film. They again took turns sleeping for two-hour shifts. Once again, the cellphone on the night table between the two beds was never turned off.

It was getting late in the afternoon on Friday when Cassidy reached Cheyenne, Wyoming's largest city and world famous for its Frontier Days rodeo.

A few exits down he turned south on I-25.

A few minutes later so did the grey RAV4.

The driver looked over to his companion.

"He's doing exactly what I thought," he said smiling.

* * *

Cassidy was on I-25 for a few hours before exiting. It was getting dark on Friday when he pulled into the driveway of a dark green two-story house set off a little on a tree-lined street in a quiet neighborhood in the Denver suburb of Mountain's Edge. He stopped behind a dark sedan and turned off the car. No outside lights were on at the house. There was a sliver of light coming through the curtains that were drawn in the front windows.

The grey RAV4 stopped down the street.

Cassidy slowly got out of the car and stretched. He reached in and pulled out the black gym bag.

In the house a man cautiously pulled back the curtains on the front windows and peered out. He saw the man walking up the driveway to the door. A second man in the living room reached for a gun on the table, chambered a round, and clicked off the safety.

"We got a visitor," said the man at the front windows.

– CHAPTER 47 –

BLACK gym bag in hand, Cassidy walked quickly past the dark sedan in the driveway, up to the front door.

He took a furtive look up and down the street. He didn't see the grey RAV4 that slowed to a stop down the street in the shadows. The driver turned off the lights. The passenger handed a pair of binoculars to the driver.

Cassidy knocked gently. A man slowly opened the door. The two men stared at each other intently. Nobody spoke. Behind the man at the door, Cassidy saw another man holding a gun at his side.

Then Cassidy broke into a broad smile. The other man chuckled. Cassidy stepped inside.

"Hello Mr. Bishop," he said as he vigorously hugged his older brother Randolph.

Bishop motioned with his head to their younger brother Joel standing behind him.

"Mr. Thornton and I have been waiting for you, we were getting a little nervous," said Bishop.

Cassidy walked into the living room just left of the front door and embraced Thornton. Bishop slammed shut the door.

"No reason to worry, my brothers, it's all good," said Cassidy as he put the black gym bag on the living room table. "Cops have no fucking clue who you are, and how we did it. I walked in to tell the cops I was going on Tuesday and they didn't say shit. Fucking idiots. So time to celebrate. Brought a little homecoming present with me to start the party."

He unzipped the bag. Bishop and Thornton looked in. There was a pile of $50 and $100 bills in neat stacks. There were several small gray bags carefully tied up and other documents.

"A few trinkets that shine, Hildy always loved her diamonds," said Cassidy, picking up a small grey bag. "Also paper that is worth a lot of dough on Wall Street."

"We got our loot upstairs, under the bed," said Thornton. "Since we got home we've been pounding a waitress broad on top of that cool $300,000 we took at the golf course."

Bishop chuckled and put his arm around Cassidy's shoulder.

"You are a fucking genius! The plan worked just as you said it would when we met you in Reno a few months ago when you snuck away from the others at the bachelor party," he said. "You just keep thinking Cassidy, just keep thinking and you will keep us rich men for the rest of our lives."

Down the street, the driver of the grey RAV4 put down the pair of small binoculars and smiled.

"I think we got him," he said to the burly man next to him. "Let's go find a place for the night. Doubt these guys will be going anywhere. They'll be too busy celebrating. Anyway, we have the tracker still on."

He started the car.

"We'll be back in the morning."

– CHAPTER 48 –

A FEW hours later, Bishop leaned back in his chair, clasped his hands behind his head and broadly smiled at his two brothers who sat around the kitchen table. He inhaled deeply on a joint.

They had spent the last few hours eating, drinking, smoking, joking, and congratulating each other on pulling off their plan and getting away scott free.

A layer of smoke floated up to the ceiling and the aroma of pot filled the room. An ashtray in the middle of the table was filled with joint butts. The table was littered with boxes of Chinese food, a half filled bottle of Jack Daniels, and empty Coors bottles. Cassidy's black gym bag sat on the countertop.

Cassidy took the joint from Bishop and took a long drag.

Nobody spoke for a few moments. Thornton got up and pulled out another beer from the refrigerator and sat down.

"Why you do it? Why you want to kill her?" asked Thornton softly.

"A cool six, eight million dollars cuts a whole lot of marriage vows and death until we part words, little brother," Cassidy said quickly, blowing out a smoke ring.

The room stayed quiet. Cassidy looked at his brothers across the kitchen table. He took a gulp from his beer bottle, inhaled on the joint, and leaned back in the chair.

"But there was more," he said softly.

Cassidy blew a cloud of smoke into the air and closed his eyes for a second.

"I was bored," Cassidy said. "Bored with my life, even with all of the big homes, ritzy cars, fancy vacations we took. Bored because it was not my life anymore. I didn't like the way my life was going. I didn't feel like I was really living anymore. It was like everything was planned out. It was like living in a movie where everything was scripted out already."

Cassidy paused, rubbed his hand through his hair and took a deep breath before he continued.

"I was in a box, that was closing in on me and sucking the life out of me. No pressure, no adrenaline rush like stepping to the 1st tee or the 18th on the last round of a tournament. On the golf course, I dictated what happened, I made a good shot, a bad shot. There was none of that."

His brothers looked at him quizzically. Cassidy just nodded his head.

He chuckled. "Even the sex. There was no more excitement, just the obligatory fuck on Saturday nights, missionary style all the time."

Thornton smiled, chuckled and said, "What did you expect, hot fucking sex. Jesus, she was like 15 years older than you."

"I don't know, she was pretty fucking sexy sitting in the basement for the taking," said Bishop with big grin.

"Whatever," said Cassidy with a shrug. "It wasn't the sex that was bothering me."

Again the room fell quiet. Thornton took a large gulp of beer and Bishop a deep drag on the joint.

"You guys have never been married, you will just keep banging bimbos your entire life. Marriage is a whole different animal. You got to keep working on it otherwise it can all fall apart in an instance," said Cassidy snapping his fingers.

"I was working it because I was getting used to having so much money around. But, at the same time I was worried because all of that money might just go away one day. Worried. It was Hildy's money. All of hers."

Cassidy paused again, took the joint out of Bishop's hand and took a drag. He slowly blew out the smoke.

"I remember the day when I knew my place. I asked her to invest in a golf course project that one of my college buddies had invited me to be part of a few years back," said Cassidy. "I think I needed like a half a million and I would have been the general manager of the course. It would have been a big deal and I could have gone back to doing something I really enjoyed. She said no. Didn't want to throw that kind of money out on something like that she said. What could I say it was her dough?"

"What about the dealership job, you were the boss, right?" said Thornton.

"Just wasn't me," said Cassidy.

Bishop got up and went to the refrigerator and pulled out another beer and sat back down.

"She told me several years ago that she was leaving most of the money in her Will to me, but a marriage and Wills can easily change," said Cassidy. "I was always living with that worry."

Cassidy took a drink of beer.

"So I decided no more Hildy, no more worry."

The brothers nodded.

"That's when I started thinking about how to do it. One thing I knew, the only people I really could trust was you guys," said Cassidy, raising his beer bottle to his brothers.

Cassidy told them how the plan began to take shape in his mind. When he was invited to the bachelor party in Reno he knew that it would be a good time to meet that would not raise any suspicion later.

"I sent you the letter so there would be no trace of email or text, told you to burn it and we met in that dumpy bar in Reno," said Cassidy.

"Once I heard your plan, I knew right away that it was going to work," said Bishop raising his beer. "When we left the bar, we went past this little casino and somebody had hit a slot machine jackpot right next to the street. Remember little brother, I told you that we would be hitting our jackpot soon."

The three brothers smiled, raised, and clinked their beer bottles.

"So here we are, waiting on a cool $2 million check from the life insurance company that the lawyer says should be coming before the end of the month," said a smiling Cassidy. "Plus, there is plenty more in the trust fund from the estate that is set up. No more worries.

– CHAPTER 49 –

POPULATION around 15,000, the small town of Mountain's Edge, Colorado is nestled at the foot of the Rocky Mountains and just a short drive from Denver. It was only beginning to stir Saturday morning with a few tables filled at the Main Street corner diner, early shoppers ducking into the supermarket, and the occasional jogger or dog walker out in the bright spring sunshine.

A grey RAV4 with NY license plates with two men in the front slowly drove down the street. They passed the volunteer fire station that was next to the red brick police station with two cruisers parked in front. The men exchanged glances.

A few minutes later, the RAV4 pulled up outside a house on a tree-lined street stopping at the bottom of the driveway, effectively blocking the exit of the two cars parked there. Before they got out of the car, both men checked the guns they had tucked into their waistbands.

"This is my play. You are back up, the muscle, no fucking around," said Garrett turning to Rudy.

As they walked past the Honda sedan in the driveway, Garrett stopped and bent down at the rear bumper. He pulled out a small tracking device from his jacket pocket and quickly attached it to the car

"Just in case they try to run later," he said. "Now let's go and say hello nice and easy."

Bishop and Thornton were sitting at the kitchen table drinking coffee. They had cleared out a little space on the table by pushing the empty beer bottles and ashtray filled with cigarette and joint butts from last night's revelry to one end.

There was a knock on the front door.

"Not expecting anybody are we?" said Bishop. Thornton shook his head. There was another loud knock.

Bishop left the room, walked cautiously to the front windows and slowly pulled back the curtain and looked out. Thornton stayed in the kitchen doorway.

"Two men," he whispered back to Thornton. "Get that shotgun ready. Who knows who the fuck they are?"

Bishop stood to the side of the front door and slowly opened it less than halfway. He peered out to face the two men.

"I'm Garrett," the first one said, lifting his jacket to show a Smith &Wesson .38 special in his waistband. "This is my colleague Rudy. We're here to talk to Cassidy."

Bishop's eyes opened a bit wider, and his Adam's apple bobbed as he took a little gulp. He looked at Garrett and then at Rudy's stone face.

Finally, he managed, "There's no Cassidy here," and started to close the door.

Garrett jammed his foot into the door.

"Don't fuck with us. We know he is here. Open the fucking door!"

Bishop hesitated a moment, taking another look at Garrett and Rudy's blank expressions. He saw a gun in Rudy's hand at his waist. Then he slowly stepped back and opened wide the door.

Garrett and Rudy walked into a little foyer with stairs leading up to the second floor ahead of them and a small dining room to the right. To the left was a bigger room with a large flat screen TV in the corner, below it an old fashioned record player and a stack of vinyl's on the floor. There was a coffee table, a sofa against the far wall and two chairs. Another man stood in the open doorway in the back wall leading to the kitchen.

The man in the doorway stepped slowly into the living room. Garrett now could see he was holding a shotgun in his right hand. Rudy raised his gun but Garrett motioned to stop.

"Ah…the third brother," Garrett said with a smile as he walked into the room and sat down in one of the chairs with Rudy in the other. "It was always a family affair."

From behind, Garrett heard footsteps on the stairs and then a familiar voice.

"You are a long way from home aren't you Detective Garrett," said Cassidy, walking into the room past the two of them and settling into the couch across from them.

Cassidy's brothers came and stood on either side of the couch. Thornton cradled the shotgun and handed a gun to Bishop. Rudy had his gun in his lap.

There was an uneasy silence in the room.

"Brothers, I would like to introduce Detective Garrett of the Cable Springs police department. This is Randolph or as you know him Bishop," said Cassidy motioning to his right. "And that fella with the shotgun is baby brother Joel, or Thornton. Detective Garrett was one of the cops looking for the kidnappers and killers of my late wife, weren't you?"

Garrett nodded.

"But, now strictly here in an unofficial role," said Garrett softly and quickly.

Cassidy raised his eyebrows.

"You aren't here to arrest us?" said Cassidy. "And your big friend?"

"He's here to look after his investment, and to get his piece of our transaction."

"His investment?"

"Me."

"Transaction?"

"We are going to do a little business together Cassidy."

"What kind of business could we do together, detective?" said Cassidy.

Garrett smiled.

"Well, you see I am in a little bit of a jam, " he said looking over at Rudy, who showed a toothy grin. Garrett told them about his $15,000 gambling debt. "I need to fix things pretty quickly.

Having you arrested won't help me with my problem or make Rudy happy. You and your newfound riches however will."

"He's got 18 days left to pay up," said Rudy, smiling. "I am here to make sure he stays alive and pays up."

"You can see my problem," said Garrett. "So you see, this is a private transaction. I am off the reservation on this one. This is strictly personal."

"You are in a shitload of trouble there Mr. Detective. Why in the hell would we even want to lift a finger to help save your ass," said Bishop, shrugging his shoulders.

Garrett let his gaze rest on each of the brothers for a moment. He sighed.

"Because with one phone call, I could haul your sorry asses into jail," he said. "Kidnapping and premeditated murder. Luckily in New York there is no death penalty. But more than likely you would rot away the rest of your sorry ass lives in jail."

Garrett waited a moment to let his words sink in.

– CHAPTER 50 –

NOBODY spoke. Garrett looked at Cassidy.

"It was a good plan. By using your brothers, you had no worry about any double cross. Not sure how you communicated but we could never find a way to connect you to them," said Garrett as Cassidy smiled. "It was almost...the perfect plan. But, I am figuring that your brother Bishop made some type of play on Hildy and your wife fought back."

He pointed to the ugly scratches on Bishop's neck.

"But all you got was that and you left a little something on Hildy's dress. A little blood. Blood type B negative to be exact. Not too many people have that type of blood," said Garrett with a slight smile continuing to look at Bishop. "But, you do. We read all about your blood type B negative in the local paper at the annual blood drives."

Cassidy shot a stare at Bishop who turned his eyes down. He turned back to look at Garrett who simply smiled.

"We could kill you here, right now," said Cassidy, as Thornton raised the shotgun and cocked the hammer. Cassidy pulled out a gun tucked in his back and placed it on the table before him.

Bishop chambered a round. "Wouldn't make any difference to us. If we have killed one, what would be two more slime balls like you matter?"

Garrett shrugged.

"There is another way around here. I would guess that you boys probably will take home more money that you ever dreamed of. You already have a cool three hundred thousand in your hands. Then there are the homes. The jewelry, paintings, the dealership whatever else your brother can get his greedy hands on. You will have so much that you won't miss giving us a little slice of the pie," said Garrett motioning with his head to Rudy.

"Now you probably could kill us both, but it doesn't really matter to me. I either come up with the money or Rudy is going to hurt me pretty bad. Probably make my life a lot easier if you just kill me right now," continued Garrett. "But before you do that, remember Rudy here is pretty fast, I am not that bad, and probably it would be safe to say that we would get at least one of you, if not possibly two of you. And we would start with you Cassidy. You want to take that chance?"

Again there was quiet. Outside a dog barked and a truck drove past.

"Now instead of most of us ending up dead, we could all walk away from here today alive and with some cash in our pockets and enjoy the rest of our lives. All we got to do is just use our heads to make a deal and not our guns," said Garrett.

Cassidy shot a look at his brothers. With his eyes he motioned for Thornton to lower the shotgun.

"What's the deal?"

"Hundred grand. We will give you 24 hours to pull it all together. You probably have that right here in the house from the 300 grand you took at the golf course," Garrett said, looking at Bishop and Thornton. "But, just in case you buried it under some tree and have to go and get it we will give you until tomorrow."

"You said you owe fifteen grand," said Cassidy, raising his eyebrows.

"A man has got to make a profit and have something to show for his work," said Garrett smiling.

"And the banker always takes a commission," said Rudy softly.

"And what do we get for our 100 grand?"

"You get my silence and my word never to hold you up again," said Garrett.

"Fuck your word. You're a dirty cop Garrett. You will always be dirty. You will keep putting the finger on me, us," spit out Cassidy.

"Once I get the 100 grand I am gone from your life. Promise. It's my word," said Garrett, raising his hand as if to take an oath.

"What about your partner Judd and that lady cop McBain? Won't they figure it out as well and come and get our asses?" said Cassidy.

Garrett told them what he did with the evidence and shook his head.

"They won't put the two and two together," he said. "Plus the Chief has pretty much closed the investigation. You are in the clear."

Garrett and Rudy stood up and slowly backed out of the room, eyes fixed on the brothers, hands on their guns until they got to the door.

"We will be back in the morning," Garrett said opening the door and walking out followed by Rudy.

The front door slammed shut and the room was quiet. Cassidy got up and quickly walked to the front windows and pulled back the curtains a little. He saw the RAV4 pull away.

"They are gone," he said turning back to look at his brothers.

"We're fucked," said Bishop. "And by a fucking lowlife dirty cop putting the squeeze on us. Fuck!"

"We are fucked because of your mistake," said Cassidy, throwing a hard stare at Bishop. "I can only guess what the fuck you were looking to do in the farmhouse with her. Shit, you never could keep it in your pants, could you?"

"Fuck, she was a good looking piece of tail, I was..." Bishop said before stopping and looking down at the floor.

"Yeah right," said Cassidy. "If you stop leading with your dick and starting using your real head we might not be in this deep shit."

"Whatever, it's over," said Thornton sharply. "What we need to do now is work out what the hell we are going to do with this cop and his big buddy."

Thornton put the shotgun on the table and the others also placed their guns down. They looked at each other.

"We got the three hundred thousand upstairs, plus I have some cash in the bag. We give them the 100 grand out of that and be done with them," said Cassidy. "As he said, we still will have plenty to go around once the life insurance check comes in, the yearly trust and more once we sell the houses and more. It's not perfect but it will do."

There was silence in the room.

"There is one other way," Bishop said picking up the shotgun. "Garrett said he was off on his own. Probably nobody knows that they are here, right?"

Bishop let the words hang in the air for a few seconds. He looked first at Cassidy and then at Thornton. The others nodded. Bishop smiled.

"When they come back tomorrow, we end it," he said.

– CHAPTER 51 –

NEARLY two thousand miles away and several hours later, McBain rubbed her eyes and leaned back in her office chair at the Cable Spring police station. She usually didn't come in on Saturdays, spending them with the family. But all through the morning while watching Steven's little league game and Stella playing soccer, she couldn't shake the troublesome feeling that she was missing something about the Hildy Swanson case.

So, even though the Chief had pretty much shut down the investigation, McBain was not ready to close the case. She had been closeted in her office for the past few hours going through the case file page-by-page still looking for something to identify and find Bishop or Thornton. The leads on Gil and Ace had turned out to be dead ends and there was no evidence that tied Cassidy to the kidnapping and killing of his own wife. Nothing.

She ran her hand through her hair and took a deep breath.

Her mentor, Morton, always said follow what you knew as fact and use that as your starting point.

What did they know?

First, that Hildy had been kidnapped and taken to an empty farmhouse on the outskirts of town on Sunday afternoon.

Second, that Hildy had badly scratched one of her abductors with her nails, whose blood was found on a piece of her dress left in the basement. The lab report identified the blood type as B negative, not commonly found in most of the population.

Other than that they could only surmise that Hildy was shot and killed in the farmhouse and then taken to the 16th hole at the golf course where she was dumped in the lake sometime Sunday night.

McBain got up and walked out from the desk to stretch her legs. Through the windows in her office, she looked out at the half empty squad room, noticing Judd was at his cubicle working on the home invasion case with Garrett's empty desk next to him. She was thinking about going to the break room to get coffee when she stopped. A nagging thought about the lab report lodged in the recess of her mind burst into her consciousness.

McBain opened the door and yelled across the squad room.

"Judd! Get in here."

Judd hurried in and sat down across the desk from McBain. There was a glow of excitement in her face.

"Didn't you tell me about finding something about one of Cassidy's brothers having an unusual blood type," said McBain.

Judd quickly opened his notebook in which he meticulously recorded every note, every step of the investigation.

"Here it is," he said, reading from his notebook. "During our background search of Cassidy's brothers, we found a Denver Post story that mentioned Randolph, the older brother. It was about a local hospital's blood drive and the fact that Randolph was a regular donor because he had a rare blood type and the local officials could always count on him."

Judd looked up from his notebook.

"Blood type B negative."

McBain looked down at the lab report.

"The blood type on the dress found at the farmhouse was B negative," she said quietly.

"Holy shit. It all makes sense now," he said.

McBain nodded and began to rifle through the case file. When she had finished, she looked at Judd.

"There is no copy of the story here," she said.

Judd shook his head.

"I don't understand," he said. "A copy of the story should be in the file."

"Not here, you sure you put it into the file," she said quietly.

"Yes," Judd said firmly. "I put everything in the file. It just didn't disappear."

McBain nodded.

"Not unless somebody made it disappear. I think I better call the Chief," she said reaching for her phone.

The Chief was not too happy about having his Saturday afternoon disrupted by McBain's call but calmed down when he heard about the possible breakthrough in the case. He said he would be at the office in a half hour.

An hour later, McBain finished briefing the Chief on the blood type match with Cassidy's older brother and the fact that the incriminating newspaper story was either missing from the case file or had been taken.

"Shit," the Chief said. "Looks like Cassidy set it all up. He uses his brothers; family blood is pretty thick so no worry about a double cross. The golf game was to throw us off the trail. They split up all the money and live happily ever after."

The Chief leaned back in his chair.

"That explains the plan, but what explains the missing evidence in the case file," he said quietly.

After a few moments of silence, McBain spoke.

"Does anybody else have a bad feeling about Garrett," she said. "Too many coincidences for my liking here."

"Come on McBain, come out with it! What are you saying?" snapped the Chief.

"First, the lab report email comes in early Monday morning, all of us are copied. Garrett is here at the office, reads it first. A little bell goes off in his head about the blood type; he finds the newspaper story in the file and puts two and two together."

"Ok, but that doesn't answer what happened to the story?" said the Chief.

Judd leaned forward in his chair.

"While there is no proof, there have been rumors that Garrett likes to gamble with the local mob and has been losing big time.

I've heard them. Nothing to substantiate but enough to think that where there is smoke there is fire," he said.

"All of sudden he sees a way out of his mess," said McBain.

"How?" asked the Chief.

"So play this out. Garrett sees Cassidy and the kidnapping money as his ticket out of his gambling troubles. Cassidy tells him is leaving the area and Garrett figures he is heading out to see brothers. He asks for some time off and follows to put the squeeze on him. It's a shakedown," said McBain.

"Garrett says fork over some dough. In return I will bury the proof that links you to the kidnapping that can land you and your brothers behind bars for the rest of your lives," she said.

The three of them looked at each other, grim faced.

"It all fits, "said the Chief as he leaned forward on the desk. "Ok, I want these bastards who killed Hildy Swanson and I want to nail Garrett as a dirty cop."

McBain nodded, looked at Judd and then at the Chief.

"We need to go to Denver," she said.

"Hell, yeah," bellowed the Chief. "You two get the first flight out of here tomorrow morning. Put the plane, car on your personal

254

credit cards. Accounting will reimburse you. Pull some cash from the emergency fund. I will put in a call to the local police in Mountain's Edge letting them know what the heck is going on and to support you out there.

"Now go get 'em!"

– CHAPTER 52 –

THERE was a slight chill in the air the next morning and Garrett was wearing a light jacket as he walked to the car in the motel parking lot.

Garrett and Rudy had again taken two-hour shifts sleeping and staying awake during the night monitoring the tracking devices left on Cassidy's and the brother's cars to make sure that they didn't try to run out of them. Still, Garrett felt refreshed and keyed up for the morning. If everything worked out as planned he could be heading home later Sunday afternoon with all the cash he needed and no more worries he thought.

At the car Garrett popped open the trunk and rummaged in the back to find a small black duffel bag. He unzipped it and pulled something out. A few minutes later he closed the trunk. If there was a chance of a gunfight come prepared for a gunfight he said to himself.

He zipped up the jacket and headed back to find Rudy in the motel restaurant for breakfast and then to check out.

A few miles away and about an hour later the three brothers were sitting quietly around the living room table, fidgeting, waiting and listening. Pistols and a shotgun were laid out on coffee table.

Bishop was the first to hear a car pull up and stop. He hurried to the front windows and opened the curtains a little to look out.

"They're here," he said.

Cassidy nodded. "You know what to do," he said quietly. "Let's do this."

Thornton got out of his chair, picked up the shotgun and went into the kitchen. Cassidy took a seat on the couch up against the living room left wall.

In the car outside, before Garrett could open the door, Rudy grabbed his arm.

"They have already killed, so what is two more dead bodies if they want to knock us off," said Rudy, as he chambered a round in his Colt 9mm.

"I know," said Garrett as he pulled out the Smith & Wesson .38 special from his waistband and laid it on his lap. "Let's go."

Garrett and Rudy walked slowly up to the house, their eyes checking the windows for any sight of movement. Even before

Garrett was able to knock on the door, Bishop opened it. He nodded and stuck his hand into Garrett's chest.

"Your guns," he said.

"No fucking way," Garrett said with a chuckle, brushing Bishop's hand away. Rudy stood silent, eyes glaring and hand at his waist. "We are coming in as we are. Now let us in."

Bishop took a big breath and nodded.

"Ok tough guy," he said.

He motioned with his hand for Garrett and Rudy to step into the living room to the left of the front door. Bishop followed and went to stand to the right of Cassidy,

"You had the night to think about giving us the cash. The quicker you can give it to us, the quicker we can leave you alone," said Garrett, his light jacket still zipped up, eying a black gym bag that was on the coffee table. "This can work for both of us, Cassidy. There is plenty of money to go around to please everybody. I hope you make the wise decision."

Cassidy nodded. As he did Garrett noticed Cassidy's eyes shift attention to behind him and to his right, where the kitchen door was. The alarm bells in Garrett's head went off.

"Shit, the other brother," muttered Garrett as he instinctively reached for the gun in his waistband.

Rudy saw the same little eye movement and with years of reading people's faces and sensing danger, instantly pulled out his weapon.

Thornton appeared in the doorway, the Remington 870 shotgun aimed at Rudy, finger on the trigger. Next came the unmistakable and frightening sound of a shotgun being racked.

Rudy swirled to get out of the chair. He raised his gun in his right hand. On instinct he squeezed the trigger, simultaneously hearing the thunder of the Remington.

The first shotgun blast hit Rudy high in his left shoulder, shattering bone and leaving the arm dangling. There was another roar. The second shotgun blast hit him squarely in the chest.

Rudy managed to get off one more shot before falling backwards. He was dead by the time he crashed into the coffee table.

Thornton felt the first bullet in his stomach and started to wobble. The second buried deep into his chest. Blood gushed out of both wounds, the Remington falling out of his hands. Thornton crumpled where he stood, the blood and life oozing out of his body.

The next few moments were a cacophony of noise, as the roar of guns was followed by the groans of the men in the room as lead found flesh and bone with deadly force.

Garrett had always been fast with the gun and he was here. He stood up and fired twice. Both bullets hit Bishop high in the chest. Bishop never got off a shot as he toppled back against the wall, blood drenching the front of his shirt.

His face contorted in pain, Bishop let out a low "ugh" as he slid down the wall. Propped up against the wall, the blood and the life flowed out of his eyes and body.

Cassidy stood up and got off three shots.

Garrett felt the first bullet from Cassidy's gun burn through his left shoulder and collarbone driving him back and off balance.

A second bullet hit Garrett in the stomach, knocking the breath out of him. More lead tore into his left thigh and blood poured from the wound. His legs buckled.

Before falling, Garrett managed to pull the trigger three more times. Two shots hit Cassidy in the chest. The third bullet missed and smashed into the wall

Cassidy wobbled a few steps. His eyes lost focus but he still thought he could see both of his brothers on the floor and motionless. He saw Garrett on his back sprawled on the floor. Cassidy saw the black gym bag still on the table and he reached for it but couldn't grab it.

Red blotches spread across Cassidy's chest as he staggered across the room and managed to pull the front door open. He stumbled down the stairs and took a few more steps on the grass before he fell on his side.

The grass was soft. He rolled on his back, his gun still in his hand. He could hear the screams of neighbors and in the distance he could hear police sirens. In the back fuzzy part of his brain, he still remembered walking into the Reno bar and telling his brothers the plan. It was a perfect plan he thought. They would be rolling in dough. It was not supposed to end like this. The sky was turning black.

– CHAPTER 53 –

THE Sunday morning early flight from LaGuardia to Denver was about half full. McBain and Judd managed to get aisle seats across from each other toward the back of the plane. Both had packed their weapons and ammunition as prescribed by TSA rules in their overnight bags that they had checked at the ticket counter.

McBain and Judd didn't speak much on the plane and after collecting their bags had hurried to pick up a rental car. Before Judd started the car, both checked, loaded and holstered their weapons.

About 45 minutes later, they pulled up outside the red brick Mountain's Edge police station on the main street. The officer at the front desk told them that they were expected and directed them to Chief Amos' office in the back.

"Not yet noon, can I get you some coffee," asked Chief Amos as he directed McBain and Judd to take seats.

Both politely declined.

"Then, what can we do for you officers? We don't usually get visitors like you in our lazy and peaceful little town," said Chief Amos with a broad smile. "Your Chief gave me a heads up that I should be expecting you and to give you all the support I could and told me that you would fill in the details."

McBain looked at Judd and nodded.

Judd went first, briefing Chief Amos on the kidnapping and killing of Hildy Swanson, the golf game and subsequent getaway of two men with $300,000 in cash.

McBain picked up the investigation with the blood test match through a Denver Post story.

"Let, me guess, it matches somebody here," interrupted Chief Amos with a grin.

"We know him as Bishop, but his real name is Randolph Cassidy," said McBain. "We believe that it was Randolph and his younger brother Joel who kidnapped and shot Hildy Swanson."

Chief Amos leaned back in his chair and smiled.

"Know the Cassidy boys," he said. "Both work in a car repair place in town. They moved here maybe two years ago from California. There was a little talk that they might have been involved in an armed robbery back there but no charges were filed. They've kept themselves out of trouble around here. Kidnapping and murder is a big step up for them. They're not the brightest boys in the world, don't see them having the brains to pull off something like this."

McBain nodded.

"Exactly. It's the third brother, RG Cassidy who we believe is the brains here of engineering the plot to kidnap and kill…his own wife," McBain said letting the final words sink in.

"His own wife…that's cold, fucking cold," said Chief Amos grimly. "Heard a little about him, but never saw him around."

"That's our guy," said Judd.

Chief Amos nodded. "Motive, money?"

McBain mouthed "millions." She finished up with the conjecture that their colleague Detective Garrett was here to extort money from the brothers to cover his gambling losses.

Chief Amos took a deep breath and rose from his chair.

"That's a pretty wild tale you tell Captain, guess we should go pay the brothers Cassidy a visit," he said.

Suddenly, the office door swung open and an excited young officer burst in.

"Chief! There's been reports of a shooting, lots of shots," he shouted.

"Calm down son, where?"

The officer gave an address.

Chief Amos turned to McBain and Judd.

"Jesus, I think that's the address of the Cassidy brothers."

– CHAPTER 54 –

WITH sirens and lights on and Chief Amos driving, they made it across town to the Cassidy house in 15 minutes. Two other squad cars were already parked in front of the house, lights flashing. Across the street, a few neighbors gathered, captivated by the frenzy of activity. A policewoman was kneeling over a body on the front lawn with the other policemen grouped around as Chief Amos, McBain and Judd jumped out of the cruiser.

"He's alive," she called, waving frantically for them to come.

The three ran over.

"Jesus, what the hell is going on?" said Chief Amos standing over the bloody body. "Who is this?"

"It's Cassidy," McBain said looking at Judd who nodded.

Chief Amos looked up at the house as an ambulance with sirens and lights on pulled up to the house.

"Get doc here and I think we are going to need more than one damn ambulance!" Chief Amos shouted to one of his men.

McBain looked down at Cassidy. His breathing was shallow and labored. His eyes were closing, the color had drained from his face, and his chest was a bloody mess. She got down on her knees. The policewoman stood up.

"Cassidy, it's McBain, stay with us, we are getting help," she said softly and pressing her hand on his chest to try to slow the blood.

Cassidy's eyes flickered.

"You?" he whispered, blood dripping out of his mouth. "Here?"

McBain nodded and put her mouth next to his ear.

"Is Garrett here," she said. "What happened?"

Cassidy swallowed and took a breath. His eyes blinked. He managed a small nod and licked his lips. McBain put her ear next to his mouth.

"Yes," mumbled Cassidy. "He came with a big guy. For the money. I shot the fucking bastard."

Cassidy managed a faint smile. McBain looked up at Judd and nodded.

"What money Cassidy," she said.

"The ransom money," Cassidy murmured, more blood coming out of his mouth.

Cassidy's eyes closed. He took a shallow breath. His head slowly rolled to the side.

An EMT pushed McBain aside. He checked Cassidy's pulse and shook his head. McBain got up. A deathbed statement with three witnesses would support a case against Garrett she briefly thought until interrupted by shouts.

"Let's go," yelled Chief Amos leading the way cautiously across the lawn toward the house.

Three uniformed cops all with guns out and McBain and Judd followed. Chief Amos slowly pushed the door open and stepped in.

The carnage was everywhere – bodies and blood filled the room.

"It's like the fucking Gunfight at the OK Corral," said Judd, eyeing the bloodshed.

Chief Amos walked into middle of the room and stopped. "Jesus."

He began to issue orders to the others.

McBain surveyed the slaughter and the bodies of Bishop, Thornton sprawled on the floor and Rudy on his back splayed on the coffee table. She went around the room kneeling down at each checking for life. There was none.

"That's Rudy, the local enforcer," said Judd standing over the body.

"So, the other two must be our Bishop and Thornton," said McBain.

Standing in the middle of the room, she looked around and then at Judd.

"Where's Garrett?"

– CHAPTER 55 –

GUNS in hand McBain and Judd followed the blood trail across the living room, stepping over Thornton's lifeless body in the kitchen doorway. There was blood splattered across the kitchen floor, down the back steps, and across the backyard. Standing on the back steps, McBain looked out and could see a man slumped under a big tree. She motioned with her head to Judd to follow her across the lawn with guns outs.

The footprints stopped about 15 feet from the tree and it looked like he had crawled the rest of the way. The man was propped up against the base of a big tree.

It was Garrett. He didn't look good. Blood was spurting out from a wound in his left thigh and there was more blood oozing from another wound in his left shoulder. His eyes were closing and his breathing was weak and forced.

McBain put away her gun and bent over him. She quickly checked his pulse and examined the leg wound. The bullet had nicked the femoral artery. She gingerly felt under Garrett's leg and found an exit hole. She turned to Judd.

"Get help quick, he's bleeding out from the leg wound, I think we are going to lose him," she said.

Judd looked down at his partner, his mouth clenched in anger.

"Fuck him," he said, pointing his gun at Garrett. "Let him die. He was my fucking partner. Now look at him. He's a disgrace to the badge."

He spit on the ground.

"He needs help now!" said McBain, looking up at Judd.

He stood still.

"Judd, we are not going to let him just die here. Go, dammit! That's an order!"

Judd looked down at Garrett, who looked blankly up at him.

"Ok," he said, holstering his gun. "We save him, but McBain, make me a promise that we are going to bury his ass in jail."

"We will, now go," said McBain.

Judd turned and headed back to the house.

McBain knelt on one knee and pressed her hand down hard on the leg wound, trying to slow the blood. She wished she had a scarf or belt that could be used as a tourniquet to stem the blood.

"Garrett, can you hear me," McBain said softly.

Garrett's eyes flickered as they focused on McBain and recognized her.

"You?" he whispered.

McBain nodded. "And Judd."

"What are you doing here," he mumbled.

"Hang in there with me Garrett, we got help coming," McBain said softly.

McBain reached behind his shoulder and found another exit wound. Another through and through shot she said to herself. McBain looked at the bullet hole in Garrett's jacket in his midsection but saw no blood. She reached down and softly touched the wound. There was something hard under the jacket. She carefully lifted up the jacket to find a bulletproof vest.

She smiled. "Very smart Garrett. You knew there was going to be trouble."

Garrett nodded weakly.

"But there didn't have to be," he mumbled in a barely audible whisper.

McBain bent down closer putting her ear next to his mouth.

"There was enough for all of us," he murmured.

"Enough of what?"

"Money," he said.

"What money?"

Garrett licked his dry lips, looked up at McBain and took a deep breath.

"From the kidnapping," he whispered. "Only wanted a little."

"Why?"

"My gambling losses," said Garrett, blinking.

"Don't die on me, Garrett!" said McBain her mouth on his ear. "Not yet."

Garrett managed a weak smile, licked his dry lips again and shook his head.

"Nobody can help," he whispered. "I'm thirsty. I'm a goner."

McBain shook her head.

"You're not going to die on me, Garrett, I am not going to let you do that," McBain said staring into his eyes. "I'm going to make you pay this time for being a bad cop, not like how you got away with the Harrigan shooting."

Garrett's eyes narrowed as he looked up at McBain, whose jaw was clenched.

"Fuck you, bitch," he spit out.

Garrett winced a little as he took a breath.

Blood was still seeping out of the leg wound and his color was draining fast from his face. McBain stood up and looked back at the house but still no Judd.

Garrett looked at McBain and grimaced.

"I'm not going to jail," he mumbled. "Fuck that, a cop in jail? I wouldn't last a day. And no bitch is going to take me in."

Garrett looked down at his bloody leg and felt the blood dripping from his shoulder down his chest.

"Finish it, McBain," he said. "Finish it now."

McBain had a puzzled look on her face. She was about to speak but Garrett cut her off.

"You want to be the good cop? Well, here's your chance," he said and with that reached slowly under his right leg and came out with his gun.

McBain sucked in a big breath.

"What the fuck are you doing Garrett?" she stammered.

"Making you finish it McBain," he said, with a faint smile.

He raised the gun toward her, finger on the trigger.

McBain didn't hesitate. Her gun came off her hip. She aimed. McBain pulled the trigger.

The bullet entered Garrett's forehead between his eyes. It made a tiny hole. Garrett made a gurgling sound; blood slipped out of his mouth, his gun fell to the ground and his head rolled to the side.

It was the last sound and move Garrett made. It was finished.

– CHAPTER 56 –

IT had taken several hours to secure the crime scene, photograph, tag and collect all the evidence, and take the bodies away to the morgue. Only then did Chief Amos drive McBain and Judd back to the station house and tell them to call their Chief and update him on the shooting.

When they had finished, Chief Amos ushered them into separate interview rooms.

McBain had lost track of how long she had been waiting before the door opened and Chief Amos, another uniformed officer, and a professionally dressed woman walked in. Chief Amos introduced them as Sergeant Martin from the county Sheriff's Special Investigations Unit and Paula Stevens, an assistant district attorney.

Once they were seated, Sergeant Martin read McBain her Miranda Rights and asked if she requested any legal representation. McBain said no and then the assistant DA indicated that the interview would be both audio and video recorded.

"What brought you and your fellow officer here," asked Sergeant Martin?

Before McBain could answer Chief Amos jumped in and briefed the others on the Hildy Swanson kidnapping and killing back in New York, the evidence tying the Cassidy brothers to the crime and the suspicions of both McBain and Judd on their colleague Garrett that brought them to Mountain's Edge.

"A dirty cop," said Sergeant Martin. "Did he tell you that is why he had come out here to get money from the kidnappers?"

McBain confirmed that she had spoken with Garrett for several minutes before the shooting and that he had admitted to coming to extort the ransom money from Cassidy from the kidnapping of his wife.

McBain took a sip of water.

"Walk us through when you shot Detective Garrett," Stevens asked.

McBain told them that yes, she was surprised when Garrett had pulled out the gun from under his body. She immediately feared for her life when Garrett pointed it directly at her with his finger on the trigger. No, she never hesitated about drawing her weapon and firing she said as her training had taught.

"He also told me that I was going to have to finish it," McBain said.

"What did she think that meant, " asked Sergeant Martin?

"That he wanted me to kill him so he wouldn't have to go to prison. He said that he knew what would happen to him as a cop in prison," McBain said.

The three nodded. The assistant DA wrote something down on her legal pad. Chief Amos opened the folder in front of him and pulled out a paper.

"Did you recognize or notice what kind of gun Garrett had?" asked Chief Amos.

McBain wrinkled her forehand and ran her hand through her hair.

"No," she said. "I didn't have time to notice that. All I knew was that he was pointing a gun at me with his finger on the trigger."

Chief Amos nodded and put the paper back in the folder and closed it.

The questioning continued for about another 45 minutes, mostly covering more on Hildy's kidnapping and some background questions on McBain and her career.

When the interview was done, Chief Amos took the other two across the hallway and walked in to where Judd was sitting and drinking a soda.

After another brief round of introductions and formalities of Miranda Rights, legal representation and the indication that the interview would be audio and video recorded, the assistant DA brusquely opened the questioning.

"Where were you and what did you see when Captain McBain shot Detective Garrett," asked Stevens as she pulled out her legal pad.

Judd did not hesitate in answering in a firm and clear voice.

"I was coming out of the house after going in to find medical help for Garrett. I saw him raise his gun directly at her," said Judd, staring intently across the table at the three. "McBain had no choice but to pull out her gun and fire. What would you have had her do, wait to see if Garrett was going to shoot her in the head or not? It was a self-defense shooting."

Chief Amos nodded and took a deep breath while the assistant DA scribbled on the pad. Judd leaned forward putting his hands on the table.

"It was a good shooting," he said, emphasizing the good. "A good shooting."

The questioning went on for another 30 minutes before the assistant DA shut off the tape and video recorder and left the room with Chief Amos and Sergeant Martin.

In the hallway the three conferred for a few minutes. Stevens was the most animated, looking several times at a sheet of paper in her hand before shaking her head and marching off. Chief Amos and Sergeant Martin talked for a few more minutes and shook hands before they split up. Chief Amos took a long breath and then went back to where McBain was sitting.

"The report will state that it was a justifiable shooting and that you feared for your life and fired in self-defense. Your colleague Judd corroborated your story," said Chief Amos. "It's never easy using deadly force, but it is part of our job. I hope that this will be the only time you need to use deadly force. Hopefully you will find some solace in knowing that it was a justified shooting."

Chief Amos continued that there would be an administrative board meeting on the incident convened in another week or so that McBain and Judd could most likely attend by videoconference. Once he had the details, he would let her Chief know.

McBain nodded and took a deep breath and slowly exhaled.

"Thank you Chief," she said.

Chief Amos extended his hand and firmly shook hers.

"Hell of a day McBain, hell of a day," he said. "Five dead in our little town in a wild west shootout. Jesus. Now it's time to get you home."

– CHAPTER 57 –

CHIEF Amos showed McBain and Judd out the back way to avoid the media already camped out in front and led them to an unmarked car for the ride to the Denver airport. He told them that he would have two of his officers hand deliver the $300,000 found under the bed, the assorted additional cash, and valuables in the gym bag to the Cable Springs police department once all of the necessary paperwork was completed in the coming days.

Returning to his office he leaned back in his chair and gazed up at the ceiling. "Hell of a day, hell of a day," he said.

In the 10 years that he had been chief, this was the proudest he had been of his little department and how the officers responded with such professionalism to the shootings.

All the pieces of the gunfight fit together except one. He turned his gaze back at the folder on his desk, sighed and opened it.

It was the report on Garrett's gun. There was no bullet chambered. The gun was empty. Garrett had shot all five rounds during the melee. In his jacket pocket was a batch of bullets.

The assistant DA had wanted to keep McBain for a few days to question her more about this matter. He had fought her on it and said it was better to let her go home and decompress a little. They could always call her back or video conference her in for the hearing. She's a good cop argued Chief Amos no reason to muddy her name or record.

"There was no way that McBain could have known that the gun was empty," he had told the assistant DA. "She feared for her life and shot. It was a good shooting."

He closed the folder and locked it away in his desk, turned, and peered out the blinds in his office at the front of the station. Three mobile TV trucks, including two from the big Denver stations, and a flock of newspaper, radio and social media outlets were camped outside waiting for him.

Chief Amos got up, put on his cap, straightened out the wrinkles in his shirt, and walked outside. "Hell of a day" he muttered to himself.

* * *

The local evening TV news was on and McBain sat on her hotel room bed at the Denver Airport Westin, wrapped in a towel, her hair still wet, from a much-needed shower, watching intently. The shooting at Mountain's Edge was the third story on.

"Five men were shot dead in a gunfight here this morning in the house behind me in the usually peaceful little town of Mountain's Edge," the Denver TV reporter said in a somber voice standing in front of the Cassidy house.

"The shootings took place at the house of Randolph Cassidy, 39, one of three brothers involved. Brothers RG Cassidy, 37, and Joel Cassidy, 32, were also dead from multiple bullet wounds. A police detective from New York, Samuel Garrett, 40, and another man from New York, Rudy Warner, 49, were also killed."

McBain took a deep sigh.

"According to Mountain's Edge Police Chief Amos, more than $300,000 in cash along with numerous pieces of jewelry, diamonds, and bonds were found in the house," said the reporter turning to Chief Amos standing next to him.

"Chief Amos what do you think happened," the reporter asked.

"A dispute turned deadly wrong apparently over money," said a solemn looking Chief Amos. "The money is believed to have been the ransom tied to the kidnapping and murder in New York of RG Cassidy's wife. Luckily, the shootings took place inside and no innocent neighbors got hurt. We have no reason believe that anybody else was involved."

McBain clicked off the TV. She got dressed and headed down to the lobby to meet Judd in the bar. "I could use a drink," she said to herself.

Judd was already sitting at the bar with a drink in hand. McBain sat down and motioned to the bartender for the same.

Judd clinked glasses with McBain. She took a long gulp and let the liquor burn going down.

"Jesus, I can't believe you shot him right in the fucking forehead," Judd said, nodding his head and smiling. "You are one hardass mother McBain!"

"Don't mess with me Judd," she said firmly. "First guy I shoot and with a head shot, imagine that. The things you can do when pushed to the limit."

There was a pause and Judd took a long drink. He turned and looked at McBain.

"I am sorry, I should have secured the area and made sure he didn't have a weapon," said Judd, shaking his head in disgust.

"It wasn't your fault," McBain said.

Judd nodded and mouthed thanks.

"It was a good shooting McBain," he said. "It was either him or you. The guy was a scumbag and he got what he deserved."

"That was the first time I ever used a gun on a person," she said quietly staring straight ahead at her reflection in the mirror behind the bar. "I have seen plenty of dead bodies shot and worse, but this was a bit different, the noise, the sound of the bullet hitting him. Not sure I want to experience that again."

Judd nodded.

"I know. It's never easy," he said. "It can really spook you and mess with your head. Maybe you might want to get somebody to talk to from the department when you get back."

Judd picked up his glass. It was nearly empty and he motioned to the bartender for a refill and one for McBain.

"He was a scumbag, wasn't he?" McBain said turning to Judd. "We thought he was dirty up in the High Country and we couldn't pin a bad shooting on him up there. But I've always known we have to deal with bad guys like him. It's our job."

She emptied her drink and picked up the refill.

Later after dinner, back in her room McBain called her husband.

"Love you. Kiss the kids for me in the morning. Have a good night. See you tomorrow," McBain said before turning off the cell phone.

She was eager to get home, to rest and glad that she had only a few hours to sleep before her early morning flight with Judd.

McBain closed her eyes and leaned back against the pillows. It had been a long and stressful day, one of madness and violence unlike any other in her life. Most days she didn't shoot a man right in the forehead at point blank range.

Garrett had pushed her, wanting her to shoot him and McBain had no doubt that if she hadn't shot first, he would have. Judd had said it was a good shooting.

She fluffed up the pillows and lay down staring at the ceiling. The shooting was still raw and vivid in her mind. It would take some time to be comfortable with the enormity of her actions she said to herself.

McBain took a deep breath and clicked off the light.

– CHAPTER 58 –

IT was Tuesday. Judd was in the office writing up the report and McBain was home resting. In the plush hallways and offices of a prestigious Manhattan law firm high above the morning din and hustle of people and vehicles on Park Avenue, the young associate knocked gently on the door of a partner and stuck his head in.

"You hear? Hildy Swanson's husband was killed in some wild shootout in Colorado on Sunday. Just read about it in the paper," he said.

A quizzical look came over the lawyer's face as he looked up from the papers on his desk.

"RG Cassidy? You're sure?"

The associate nodded and put a copy of the NY Times on his desk, opened to a story about Cassidy's death.

"Take a look," he said.

The lawyer quickly read the newspaper story. When he was done, the associate put a folder on the desk.

"The Hildy Swanson folder," said the associate. "Figured you would be wanting to look at it now."

The lawyer nodded and motioned with his hand for the associate to leave and close the door behind him. For the next hour, the lawyer went through Hildy's Will, scribbling notes on his legal pad. When he was done, he leaned back in his chair and smiled.

"I remember now. Hildy, you were very smart, " he said under his breath.

The lawyer hit the speaker button on his desk phone and dialed the extension for the associate.

"Need you in my office now. We got work to do," he said.

* * *

No family members had claimed the Cassidy brothers, so the city had taken care of the final arrangements. On a sunny spring Friday later that week, a caravan of hearses pulled out from the county morgue and headed to the small cemetery on the outskirts of Mountain's Edge where three plots had been dug.

Garrett would be buried next to his favorite uncle back in Buffalo and Rudy's boss had sent somebody out to bring back his body.

Two of the Cassidy brothers' co-workers from the auto body shop and the waitress who slept with both of them were the only mourners to watch as the bodies were lowered into the ground. The police department Chaplin said words over them. Small markers with their names at the head of the graves were the only signs of who was buried beneath.

Chief Amos watched silently and when the last coffin was lowered in and the dirt was being shoveled, he nodded, turned away, and headed to his car.

* * *

McBain had spent the week at home resting and relaxing as ordered by the Chief. She took care of some long ignored chores around the house, tended her little garden, and took some extra long walks with Buster on the dog's favorite paths. She went to see the police therapist one afternoon. For the most part with the house empty, McBain would simply lounge on the deck, close her eyes and let the warm spring sun melt away the memory of squeezing the trigger and seeing the small deadly hole appear between Garrett's eyes.

The following Monday, McBain walked into the squad room greeting the others with a smile and big hellos.

Officer Bonner told her "good job" as she walked past. It was the same from the others. She sensed a different level of recognition and even respect from them she thought. It felt good.

Judd looked up from his desk, smiled, and nodded. She was grateful how, in the hours after the shooting, he had soothed her worries about the validity of the shooting, repeatedly telling her that it was a "good shooting."

This case and the events of that afternoon in Mountain's Edge had changed the dynamics of their working relationship. Afterwards, she had come to a fuller appreciation of his level of professionalism and empathy for his colleagues.

There was a vase of flowers on her desk when she entered her office. A small, gift-wrapped package was also on her desk.

She smelled the flowers and read the handwritten note:

"McBain, Enjoy the flowers. You did your job." – Morton

She sank into her chair and leaned back. She looked out at the squad room at Garrett's empty desk. It was like he had never been there, wiped off the department's ledger for good.

Now, she thought it was time to move on and get back to work.

Later that day at County Hospital a letter arrived on Dr. Steiner's desk. He noticed the return address was from a high-powered law firm based in the city.

It read:

To: Dr. Stuart Steiner

Re: Estate of Hildy Swanson

My law firm represents Hildy Swanson's estate and is executor of her will.

This letter is to notify you that Elsa's Room for Infectious Diseases at County Hospital is the sole beneficiary of Hildy Swanson's trust after the death of her husband RG Cassidy.

Please have your office contact me to set up a meeting at your earliest convenience to discuss details.

Dr. Steiner put the letter down, turned in his chair to look out at the window on the sun-drenched lawn and trees behind the hospital.

His thoughts turned to Hildy and her promise to one day to be buried next to her younger sister Elsa. One promise kept.

He remembered her second promise that her financial support for the hospital and his department would carry on in life and in death.

"All promises kept and more, Hildy," he said.

THE END

Made in the USA
Middletown, DE
20 April 2024